W0232630

PENGUIN BOOKS
THE LEGENDS OF PENSAM

A journalist and former civil servant, Mamang Dai was born in
Pasighat in the East Siang district of Arunachal Pradesh. Her
published works include *Arunachal Pradesh: The Hidden Land*
and *River Poems*.

Mamang Dai lives in Itanagar.

the legends of pensam

mamang dai

PENGUIN BOOKS

An imprint of Penguin Random House

PENGUIN BOOKs

USA | Canada | UK | Ireland | Australia
New Zealand | India | South Africa | China | Singapore

Penguin Books is part of the Penguin Random House group of companies
whose addresses can be found at global.penguinrandomhouse.com

Published by Penguin Random House India Pvt. Ltd
4th Floor, Capital Tower 1, MG Road,
Gurugram 122 002, Haryana, India

Penguin
Random House
India

First published by Penguin Books India 2006

Copyright © Mamang Dai 2006

All rights reserved

10 9 8 7 6 5 4 3 2

ISBN 9780143062110

This is a work of fiction. Names, characters, places and incidents are either the
product of the author's imagination or are used fictitiously, and any resemblance
to any actual person, living or dead, events or locales is entirely coincidental.

Typeset in *Minion Regular* by SÜRYA, New Delhi

Printed at Manipal Technologies Limited, India

This book is sold subject to the condition that it shall not, by way of trade
or otherwise, be lent, resold, hired out, or otherwise circulated without the
publisher's prior consent in any form of binding or cover other than that in
which it is published and without a similar condition including this condition
being imposed on the subsequent purchaser.

www.penguinbooksindia.com

This is a legitimate digitally printed version of the book and therefore might not
have certain extra finishing on the cover.

For my parents
Odi & Matin Dai

For my parents
Olli & Marja D.H.

In our language, the language of the Adis, the word 'pensam' means 'in-between'. It suggests the middle, or middle ground, but it may also be interpreted as the hidden spaces of the heart where a secret garden grows. It is the small world where anything can happen and everything can be lived; where the narrow boat that we call life sails along somehow in calm or stormy weather; where the life of a man can be measured in the span of a song.

contents

author's note

◄◄◄◄◦►►►►

Arunachal Pradesh in North East India, bordering Bhutan,
China and Myanmar, is one of the largest states of the country,
and also one of its greenest. It is the homeland of twenty-six
tribes with over one hundred and ten sub-clans, each with a
different language or dialect. Part of the Eastern Himalaya, the
land is criss-crossed by rivers and high mountain ranges running
north-south that divide it into five river valleys. The mightiest
of its rivers is the Siang, known as the Tsangpo in Tibet, and
the Siang valley, stretching northwards to the Tsangpo gorge
where the river enters India, is the territory of the Adi tribe
who are the subject of this book.

Like the majority of tribes inhabiting the central belt of
Arunachal, the Adis practice an animistic faith that is woven
around forest ecology and co-existence with the natural world.
There are few road links in their territory. Travel to the distant
villages still entails cumbersome river crossings, elephant rides,
and long foot marches through dense forest or over high
mountain passes.

But the old villagers who walk miles every day say: 'When
you look at the land you forget your aches and pains.' And it

really is a beautiful landscape. So far, isolation has been the best protection for the pristine forests and rich bio-diversity of Arunachal Pradesh. Though a number of tourist circuits have been opened since 1992, the state still maintains entry formalities of an Inner Line and Restricted Areas Permit for visitors.

prologue

The helicopter ploughs through the clouds. For a moment it lifts, then seems to take a nose dive as a current of air hits it. I wrap my arms around the empty seat in front of me.

There are six of us in the ageing, struggling machine and everyone is silent or pretending to be asleep. Below us, the big river is calm, frozen between shoals and sandy flats as if locked in a trance.

All the river systems, in fact, are calm; streams of glass spread across the earth like lost pieces of a shining ocean. The first line of hills beyond the plains of Assam is a strip of dark green jungle. Here, the narrowest, deepest ravines have wedged themselves in between each twisted and pitted hill. Higher mountains loom ahead, where the earth has been pushed up and folded into a knot of jagged peaks.

Soon, the flat lands disappear. There are no more roads. We gather speed. The clouds race with us. They race past and ahead of us, drawing us into the hidden valleys of my home.

~

I was born in the mountains, in a village where boys kicked rocks around pretending at football. Every time a vehicle drove up to the school-house, there was great excitement, and we flew over the warm stones, thundering down to the edge of the field where we skidded to a halt and stood trembling with curiosity under the old jackfruit tree.

The years circled us as if in a dream. Very few strangers crossed our paths. Every evening we sat on the bamboo veranda, my clan sisters and brothers and I, and gazed at the stars whose names we made up according to their configurations. The root of light was the plough, I remember. Or was it the lady who competed with the gods to weave a tapestry? Now it matters little, except that in those days when we looked at the stars we felt that they were very close and that their fire shone directly on us.

Back then, the village heaved with life, and I expected a great welling up of revelations, a web of magic through which we would step lightly like glittering spirits crowned with speech and thought. The years stretched before us like a singing forest; we were always poised to spread wings and float through the cool bamboo.

We make no comparisons now. The river cuts through our land as before in its long journey to the sea. In spring the red flowers still blaze against our sky. But the old people now, the few of them alive, turn slowly in their sleep as the fires burn down to a heap of ash. In the middle of the night a bird swoops low and calls out in a wild, staccato note. The thatch rustles. The bamboo creaks. The darkness is full of breath and sighs.

The rain comes gently, bathing the night. And sometimes, behind the curtain of rain, I see names and faces rising up like obscure jewels, shining again in their singular paths and destinies.

a diary of the world

We have long journeys in our blood

a diary of the world

We have long journeys in our blood

the boy who fell from the sky

◄◄◄◄◉►►►►

When Hoxo first opened his eyes to the world, he saw green. A green wall of trees and bamboo, and a green waterfall that sprayed his cheek and washed the giant fern that seemed to be waving to him.

They were moving very fast. He was being carried on the back of a man whom he was later to call his father. All he knew at this moment was that he was strapped in a basket that was hard and scented with sweat. He could feel the strength of the man; with his head pressed against the wide back, he listened to the sound of a big heart thumping as they trotted silently through an unknown land.

Hoxo would never recall the events before that journey through the great trees. When he spoke about the world, about men and forests, he thought he could taste salt and blood and sense the terror of free fall, but he was not certain why this was so. In his dreams he saw a blazing sun that spun earthwards and exploded in a burst of red fire, blinding him with blood and ash, and that was why, he thought, maybe, his eyes had been shut tight, as though he preferred the darkness to that terrifying light.

The colour green always soothed him. It was the colour of escape and solitude. He could not tell what it was that he had escaped or when, nor could he understand his need to trek into the forest sometimes to be alone.

When they reached the house on the hill, a woman had run out to greet them. He instantly recognized her as someone kind and good. She was tall and young and her face was vivid with love and anxiety.

'Oh, my!' she had said. 'A baby boy!'

She lifted him out of the basket. Even today Hoxo could not remember any happiness greater than the moment of that touch he had known more than half a century ago.

Hoxo immediately sensed there were no other children in the house. He had no idea how old he was, no one said anything, and no one ever asked him if he loved his father more or his mother, like he heard all the other children being asked. When he joined school, the children there stared at him. No one greeted him and he remembered his own tentative smile full of hope and eagerness. Rakut was his first friend.

'Here, catch!' Rakut threw him a stone that arced through the distance between them. It was a flat river-stone that Rakut had specially chosen for them to play with. Theirs was a wonderful friendship. When Hoxo's mother made rice cakes and called his friends, Rakut would be the first to arrive, grinning like an idiot, while Hoxo could hardly eat anything because he was so happy and full of pride for his parents' generosity. Once, when his father brought home a red squirrel, Hoxo ran all the way to Rakut's house shouting at the top of his voice for him to come and see it. Every day the boys found something new. Every day they explored the hills further and further away from the village, and every day, for many years, they climbed to the flat top of their favourite hill and flung themselves down on the open ground just talking and speaking their thoughts to the trees, the cane bushes and the sharp summer light.

One day Hoxo ran all the way again to call Rakut to come and hear something strange. The two boys tiptoed around the house and lifted themselves at full stretch to peer through the cracks in the bamboo posts.

'It was real, I tell you,' Hoxo's father was saying. 'I heard a splash and when I turned I saw the edge of the river lifted up and the waters falling off the back of this long shining fish... or snake...whatever it was! Then immediately it was gone. But I saw it, I tell you!'

'Tah! How can it be!'

'I tell you, I saw it!'

'What did it look like?'

'I thought I saw a head with horns.'

'What!'

Everyone present knew the story of Biribik, the water serpent. No one, for generations now, remembered the name of the first person who had seen it, but the event was fixed in their collective memory. It had happened on a night of heavy rain when a fisherman was alone with his nets by the river. He heard a rushing sound as the waters parted and then suddenly, when he looked up at the tree he was sheltering under, he saw a serpent coiled up in the branches looking down at him with ancient eyes. What shocked him the most was the fact that the serpent had a head with horns. The fisherman ran for his life, all the way back to the village, but as everyone could have predicted he never recovered from the effects of that terrible vision. Within a year, he had died of a wasting illness.

Anyone studying the signs could understand that something unnatural was bound to happen again, now that Hoxo's father had seen the serpent. In these small clearings in the middle of the forest, people have premonitions. Women dream dreams. Babies are born who grow up unnaturally fast, like deer or lion cubs. Infant mortality is high. Old women still braid threads of vine and pray for safe passage.

So no one was surprised when Hoxo's father was killed in a hunting accident shortly afterwards. A tragedy was expected. Ever since the arrival of firearms into these hills, hunting had become a passion. Suddenly, on any given day, a man would stand up, stretch himself, pick up his gun and walk off into the forest. Many of the hunters disappeared for days, huddled in a machan or perched, alert, on a broad branch. In the forests beyond the village where the hunters fanned out to go their separate ways, Hoxo's father was mistaken for prey. Deer? Bear? The distraught man who shot him could not say. He only remembered a movement, a dark shape that he swore was definitely not human. He had heard a piercing scream of shock and rage afterwards and had rushed headlong into the thorny undergrowth to find his friend shot through the tender point just below the jaw. He was spilling blood and his eyes were staring wide.

'Hai...I am killed!' He was crouched low and his gun was pointing into the ground. It was propped against his shoulder because his right hand had also been shot away.

His friend shouted and cried, running through the forest like a madman. 'Help me! Help me!' The cries sent a shudder through the village. Everyone rushed out. 'Help me carry his body!'

They worked all night, lifting the dead man and carrying him through the forest, dragging the body, pushing it, cursing and crying, sliding down the hill over the wet leaves and oozing mud. By the time they reached the village the men were torn and bruised and splattered with mud and the blood of the dead man. It was a frightening sight. Hoxo's mother ran out screaming. Dazed out of sleep, the young Hoxo had a vision of her flashing through the air like an incandescent flame. He understood everything, and the secret of love revealed itself to him in that one instant when he saw her embrace the inert body and press her cheek against the shattered head.

Then she said, 'Cover him. Carry him in.'

The punishment for killing a man is death, unless a meeting can be called immediately and the aggrieved party is convinced that the matter is negotiable. In this case the poor friend was banished to live like an animal in the forest for a whole month. His closest kin could take him cooked food but there were so many taboos on the type of food he could eat that it was simpler to let him fend for himself. No one opposed the exile, least of all the man whose fate it had been to mistake a man for prey.

The one thing no one could explain at the time, or at any time later, was the small fish that was found in the dead man's shirt pocket. It was slippery and mashed and the scales stuck to his skin even when they ripped open the shirt and tried to wipe away the blood. Maybe it was a fish he had caught in one of the small streams. Maybe it was something he was bringing back for Hoxo. Or maybe it was the spirit manifestation of something else. Who could tell about these things?

And so it was. The death of Lutor, famous chief of the Ida clan, father of the boy who fell from the sky, was mourned far and wide. And Hoxo's mother became one more widow in the village where so many young women had lost their men in hunting accidents.

the strange case of kalen, the hunter

◄◄◄◄◉►►►►

On one of my visits to the big city, I mentioned this village in passing to my friend Mona. She is a magazine editor, always looking for an interesting story, and she decided immediately to come with me to Gurdum town, where I lived. From there we would travel together to the village of widows.

It was early summer when Mona and I arrived in Duyang, which is also my late mother's ancestral village. We climbed up the hill to meet Hoxo and his family. Hoxo's house was as I remembered it, always full of people. There were his two sons and their wives—and now, their five children—as well as friends, brothers, sisters and relatives who came and went at any time, just to talk, gossip or to sit on the veranda sipping black tea and rice beer. Day or night, the fire was always burning and the enormous pots and pans with heavy lids were full of food or contained enough leftovers to feed another ten people. There were always visitors who appeared out of the blue, dusty and full of stories about the journey: the rutted roads, the boat crossing, the thinning jungle.

When we had climbed the hill to the house, a woman came out to greet us. It was Losi. My late mother had told me stories

about Hoxo and her, and how they had met and finally got
married—the boy who fell to earth, and the girl born to the
river woman. Everything about Losi's manner, her smile, her
eyes, suggested warmth and innocence. Then Hoxo's mother
emerged, squinting in the strong sun, and like Hoxo when he
first saw her, and like me, Mona too fell under her spell. She
was very old now but her mind was sharp and alert. She was
quiet when I told her about Mona's interest in the stories of the
village. Then she nodded and said that if this was what our
guest wanted, maybe we would be interested in hearing a story
her grandson Bodak had to tell.

In this way, we heard the strange tale of Kalen.

It had happened quite recently and was still spoken of only in
hushed tones. Kalen had been ill with malaria for weeks. Every
time the fever seized him he would cry out in rage and shout
that he would find a medicine to beat the fever, just you wait.
Then he would huddle up in bed, shaking and sweating until
the fever eased and he looked around him with calm eyes
again. One morning a group of men decided to set out on a
hunt. For many days they had been staking out an area where
the deer came to feed on the wild fruit that littered the forest
floor. It was a mild summer morning, and Kalen started out
with them saying that he needed the exercise and the fresh air.

The men were following the rules of the kiruk, a chosen
number beating an area to drive out animals while others
waited in ambush, guns at the ready. Towards noon the men
saw a group of screeching, chattering monkeys shaking the
branches of the trees across the stream that marked the
boundaries of their hunting area. It was an unusual sight, as if
the monkeys, moving upstream, jumping from tree to tree,
were waving and calling out to the men. The hunting party

decided to fan out and follow the arboreal band. It was not clear exactly who had decided to go or stay, but Bodak recalled that everyone had begun moving upstream along the right bank almost at the same moment. So he was quite surprised to see Kalen suddenly emerge from the undergrowth of the opposite bank, where the monkeys were.

Bodak started back, but Kalen signalled for him to be quiet. Bodak noticed that Kalen was wearing his old fur cap— maybe because he had only just recovered from the fits of fever—and that he had a peculiar, challenging sort of smile, as if he dared anyone to try and stop him. Bodak guessed that he must be thinking of how monkey meat was good for the blood and how it was believed to cure malaria. So he said nothing at the time but urged Kalen to cross the stream quickly so that they could move up together. Kalen motioned for him to go ahead, indicating that he would be right behind him. Shortly after this, the bright afternoon suddenly faded. The band of monkeys disappeared. And Bodak felt the jungle starting to steam with buried warmth as an oppressive silence settled on it.

Every member of that ill-fated group said later that they had all been astonished when a thunderclap broke the silence and rain began to pelt down. The skies had been clear only a moment ago! As they ran for cover they heard a loud shriek and immediately knew that something unfortunate had befallen them. Bodak remembered that he had shouted loudly, calling out to everyone to be careful and to disclose their positions. Everyone was there except Kalen. The man called Loma stood stock still with his gun and said that he had just fired at a monkey on the opposite bank. Without a word Bodak rushed back down the stream and all the men ran after him. As they splashed across madly, they saw Kalen slumped against a tree. It was raining heavily and blood was pouring out of him. His body had been ripped almost to shreds by the bullet that had exploded inside him. The men did what they could, which was not much, and while one runner was sent to inform the village, the others lifted Kalen and headed towards the cane bridge further downstream so that they could bring the body home in a somewhat intact condition.

It is unimaginable how unwieldy and terrifying the body of a dead man can be, Bodak said. The body slipped and the men choked and shuddered as the torn limbs threatened to come apart in their arms. When they reached the bridge, Bodak and Loma carried the body ahead while the others followed with their guns and Kalen's headgear. Just when Bodak had crossed the bridge with the body, the cane lashings came undone and the bridge swung and sagged in the middle, toppling the rest of the men into the stream. It was a cursed afternoon. The villagers lit bamboo flares and waited all night to receive the men who returned ill and dazed, as if they had come back from the realm of malevolent spirits.

Kalen's widow, Omum, now lived with his parents. She had two small children and was barely in her mid-twenties. When we saw her, she was still wearing her hair tied back in colourful bands like a gymnast. She fetched water, lit the evening fire, fed the pigs and chickens and carried on with her life without stopping to pine or utter recriminations.

The village, too, carried on. Like Omum, it was resilient in an unconscious way, as if programmed to be so. In the midst of injury and death, newly-weds fought, stormed out of their homes, deserted the children and hurled abuse at one another, as if the business of living and loving was a temporary arrangement. They came back after a month or two looking nervous and sheepish, and finally settled down to a kind of heaving, unpredictable domestic life, cursing and laughing.

But there were always the few who never returned. Their rage and confusion carried them so far away, beyond the mountains and down the river, that those they left behind learned to live without them. Sometimes they were remembered in songs and stories, like the dead.

the silence of adela and kepi

⋘◉⋙

Losi was cooking a feast for us, and sitting on the bamboo
veranda with Hoxo and Mona, looking out into the evening
smoky with wood fires from the houses huddled together, I felt
that all of the world that I would only read about could be
reproduced in this dusty village with its one road. Just as all the
loves and births and accidents of this habitation in the forest
could be enacted anywhere else. People everywhere made peace
in all sorts of ways, and coped until fate cut them down or
lifted them up.

Hoxo's mother came out with rice beer for us and sat next
to Mona. Already, a strange bond had grown between them. I
could see that Mona had been affected deeply by something,
and when Hoxo's mother turned to me and said, 'Tell us about
our guest, is she a mother?' Mona understood. 'Tell them,' she
said, 'tell them to pray for my daughter.'

Mona is of Arab-Greek extraction and her husband Jules is
French. They are a powerful, successful couple by any estimate—
he a famous development scientist and she the proprietor of a
glossy magazine, *Diary of the World*, that carries unusual true-

life stories. They have what I call a mobile lifestyle; they move across countries and continents and were at that time on a brief posting in New Delhi.

Jules travelled more than Mona. It was during one of his long tours that Mona, alone in their apartment, suddenly realized that something was wrong with their three-year-old daughter. They had hired a maid, a middle-aged widow from Garhwal, and given her the small room at the top near the fire escape. The woman was sturdy and she performed all her duties without any cause for complaint. Mona's daughter, Adela, loved the maid and the two got on so well together that Mona began to leave the house for longer and longer periods to pore over her papers and peer into her computer at office. Then, one day, her daughter refused to speak.

Mona crouched down beside her and tried to get her to utter a word, and the girl stared back at her for a long minute and then turned away as if she had never seen Mona before in her life.

For the next few days Mona tussled with her child.

'My baby! Tell me! Tell me what has happened to you!' she cried, shaking the girl to get a reaction.

She went to doctors and consulted her relatives and friends. She rang her mother and tried to retrace their family history. No, there had never been anything like it before. There was no history of any illness like asthma or autoimmune disease in the family that could be linked to autistic behaviour, because by now little Adela was being diagnosed with the mysterious condition of autism.

Jules came back and they quarrelled bitterly.

'*She* must have done something!' Mona raged, accusing the maid who fell on her knees and wept.

'What's the good of saying that now!' Jules shouted at her.

The words struck Mona like a slap in the face. Jules's manner and tone seemed to imply that it was her fault and she was so angry and hurt by this that she thought she would spit on his face and walk out of the house for ever.

'*He* was the one always travelling around the world. There were so many times he could have skipped a meeting but he never did.' Every time she remembered those terrible days, Mona was close to weeping with rage.

Finally, they had put Adela in a school for autistic children. They trembled with fear and sorrow when their child was seated behind a desk and given paper and crayons. The woman in charge told them that there were many cases like theirs; they should be brave.

'I just want my baby back,' Mona said when I had finished, and looked at Hoxo and his mother, wanting them to understand. 'I just want to be a mother again.' She said that when she dropped something or bumped against a table or cried, her child laughed without any feeling.

Hoxo had listened to us in silence. Now he said, 'Some things are beyond recall, and such things happen all the time. It is better to be ready.'

Then he told us of the tragedy that befell the Karyon Togum family at about the same time that little Adela withdrew from the world.

~

It happened in the playground at the edge of the neighbouring village of Yabgo. Togum's son had just crossed two years then. A cough had been rattling in the boy's chest, so his mother had bundled him up in his father's woollen scarf and put him on the back of the young girl they had hired to help out with the housework. He looked cozy strapped to the girl who was, maybe, only eleven or twelve years old herself. The young girl muttered cooing words as she set off to stand around with the other children in the playground, all of whom carried younger siblings securely fastened on their backs with shawls and cane straps. They jumped around, making a good racket like children should. They made spinning blades out of the jack-tree leaves and ran in between the houses and raced over the mud and stones. Old widow Dajer, spinning cotton in her dim house, was the only one annoyed by their exuberance.

'Watch out you don't fall!' she shouted angrily.

Late that evening the child was burning with fever. Mother and son spent a fitful night lying near the fire and in the morning she noticed how still the boy was. She was a practical woman and did not want to rush him to the general hospital. Children had all kinds of ailments, she knew that, and she had nursed two daughters already. But she was worried. When the child's condition did not improve, the parents finally decided to take him to the hospital in Pigo. They left early in the morning, by the only bus that took the road at the base of their hill. It took them till noon to get to the town. The regular doctor was away, so they had to wait for the new doctor to see them. It was very late by the time it was their turn, but the doctor was kind. He prescribed some tablets and instructed a nurse to give Kepi, the little boy, an injection. Then he said that the boy must be kept warm and in bed for a week, after which they were to bring him back.

Kepi seemed to improve after this. His mother fed him mashed rice and warm water and he opened his mouth and ate everything she gave him. But at night he cried out in a high-pitched wail that filled her with an icy fear. One morning the boy's father, Togum, noticed a dark bruise mark on his upper arm. It had probably been there all this time but they had mistaken it for a mark left by the strap of the basket he was carried around in and had paid little attention to it in the tension of running to the hospital and watching over him at night. When old Dajer came around to visit she said crossly that the way all the children had been playing and running about the other day, she wouldn't be surprised if the maid had dropped the child. When they questioned the maid she admitted that she had slipped and fallen but that the baby had not fallen off at all. They had just landed together with a thud on the ground. That was all.

Togum did not speak to his wife all of that day and night, till she shouted at him for holding her responsible for their misfortune. The next morning he put his hand on her arm without a word and she understood the fear that he too was hiding and she forgave him.

Quietly, slowly, the days passed. Children are the life of a family and by now terror had seized everyone. Hai! The entire village rallied to the aid of the parents who watched their child open his mouth wide and emit silent cries. Kepi's mother wept and quailed at the touch of his lips against her fingers when she fed him. Togum moved around as if he was drugged, nodding silently to everyone who came. On the advice of relatives many rituals were performed. Togum travelled far and wide in search of famous shamans. A year passed. The child did not move during all this time but he cried, ate, and slept with his small torso twisted stiff and unmoving. They carried him everywhere. Then someone said that they should think about performing a special ceremony, rarely performed these days, in case it was the spirit of a snake that had coiled around the body of their son.

It was Hoxo who was called to conduct the ceremony. He

told us now how he saw it all quite clearly. He saw Togum leave on a sunny morning for the timber depot in the middle of the forest where he had been felling trees. The logs were still lying in a pile and an elephant had been hired for the day to move the logs to the platform above the trench where they could be marked and sawed. The workmen were talking loudly and moving towards the woodpile when the elephant stopped dead in its tracks. No amount of cajoling, prodding or threats would move the beast to take another step forward. It dawned on the frustrated men that maybe a snake had made its home among the logs. What else would frighten a tusker standing nine feet tall and with the strength to kill them all if it wanted to?

Togum thought it might be a king cobra. They couldn't see anything and they dared not move the logs. The ferocity of the cobra is legendary and it is known to attack without provocation. There had been many instances of this snake rearing itself up and running after some unfortunate man. Once its fangs had hit, it would keep pumping its jaws, injecting as much venom as possible into the victim.

All night Togum lay awake thinking about logs and elephants. He heard his wife sighing and he thought he heard the rustling of leaves. He saw a full moon rising. He wondered what he should do. They lived in the forest surrounded by animals of every kind, but unlike many of his friends Togum had no experience of hunting and he did not want to kill. He prayed that if there was indeed a snake in the pile of logs, it would move away during the night.

The next morning, he put on his old hat and armed himself with his shotgun reluctantly. He hoped he wouldn't have to use it. He carried only two cartridges.

They coaxed the elephant again but the creature still refused to budge. Togum positioned himself and crouched by the logs for a long time. There was no movement. The rest of the men and the elephant had moved into the shade and Togum could feel his back burning. Suddenly his eyes were dazzled by an iridescence that took his breath away. It was gold, it was green, it was dark amethystine and changing and shining with an indescribable beauty. In a flash he pointed his gun and fired at this vision that had exposed itself so suddenly, trapped in a ray of sunlight. The shot blinded him. There was a thud as a log splintered and pieces of wood flew in all directions. The men rushed forward but the iridescence had vanished. They waited again. There was no movement and everything was still and silent as before. By now the men were impatient and edgy.

'Come on, let's try moving the logs,' one of them said, and cursing and spitting they began to heave and roll the logs while Togum pointed with his gun again. Every nerve and muscle in his body was tense. He was not thinking of anything, just waiting and at the ready, praying he should not miss. Then he saw a frightening sight. With every movement of the logs an enormous coiled python unwound itself loop-by-loop, rearing and twisting fiercely. And the horrifying thing Togum remembered forever afterwards was the absolute silence of the snake, its body torn in the middle by the gunshot, still struggling, the afternoon light shining into the vertical pupils of its yellow eyes. Togum held his breath. He felt the hairs prickling on his head and almost in reflex he fired at the rotating head. He was lucky. The shot blew the head away. And although the body of the snake continued to heave Togum saw the fabulous shimmer dim right before his eyes even as the sunlight and the green forest around him seemed to dwindle and fade.

'This was why,' Hoxo told us, 'the serpent ritual had to be performed. But sometimes it is a matter of time, too.' He said that all night they had chanted and negotiated with the spirits, calling them to restore the sick child, but the spirits had moved away to a place beyond recall. 'They are the most dangerous ones, the ones who go away and never return,' he said.

Mona and I listened. I knew the story well, just as everyone else in the village did. 'These things happen all the time,' Hoxo said. 'We only begin to know about them when they happen to us.'

Hoxo kept talking like this. He seemed to live in a timeless zone and from a great distance, sitting in this village house, in his green galuk and khaki shorts, he followed his interests in the lives of men, animals and plants, in the origin of the universe, or quite simply thought about how to be a good chess player. It was as if he would never be surprised by any condition or behaviour of man or beast. When I had spoken of Adela's autism, he had listened and understood, and been able to express his sorrow for Mona quietly. Whereas I had had to look up the term in the library when she first told me. I had been too troubled and agitated to share her grief.

The two children had this in common: they both loved music. At the centre for autistic children in the big city, Mona and Jules had stood still as the voices of children rose and wavered in a strange cacophony that brought tears to their eyes. Then they had watched their daughter beat a small drum and smile lopsidedly, and they had been comforted. In the village, Togum's little boy lay in bed all day and listened to radio music that filled every corner of the house. His sisters and their friends crowded round him and pulled funny faces and gave him a little pat sometimes, even though no one was sure whether he recognized them or not.

It was the same every time I came to visit the family. When I took Mona to meet them, the radio was playing and the boy's mother smiled as she greeted us. She was young and robust. Togum, who was lean and dark, rose from his corner and said, laughing, that he was the babysitter now since the new maid had gone home for a while. We drank bitter tea. The wife did everything and Kepi's sisters, who were skinny-legged adolescents now, shuffled and bumped into each other till the mother shouted for them to leave the house and let us talk in peace.

And I saw again how their days were passing: the fire burning brightly in the hearth, the dogs curled up close to the flames, the cot in the corner. Life moved on quite normally, except that like so many others in so many unseen recesses all over the world, they hid their pain, while the seasons turned.

pinyar, the widow

◀◀◀◉▶▶▶

Pinyar, the widow was drying clothes by the fire when Mona and I went to see her. As usual, she was grumbling and cursing, shaking the wet clothes with an angry thwack. Thwack! Thwack! Pinyar had been widowed when she was not yet twenty-five, in the third month of her marriage to a good-hearted man with whom she had hoped to make a new life.

Before that, she had borne a son to another man, one she had lived with for some five years. His name was Orka, and he had come to her from a village beyond the Siyum hills, far to the north of the country. He was a big, handsome man with laughing eyes and he had swept the young Pinyar off her feet. Her family had opposed the liaison, saying quite openly that the clan of Orka was no good, they were trouble. But nothing could convince Pinyar, and one day she announced that she was pregnant with Orka's child.

Her family called all the elders to negotiate and solemnize the marriage. Orka, however, skirted the issue, and though he acknowledged paternity, within a year of the birth of their child he was preparing coldheartedly to abandon Pinyar.

They had named their child Kamur. When he left for his

village, Orka took Kamur with him, for the child was a son. Though he said he would return, he never did. Pinyar bowed her head in shame. But by all the laws of her clan she alone was to blame for her misfortune and there was nothing anyone could do about it.

Some years later, her life seemed complete again when she became the wife of Lekon. Her family advised her to nurture this relationship and behave with propriety, but soon after they had married Lekon was struck down one evening in a hunting accident.

That had happened some twenty years ago. Now Pinyar lived alone and worked in the fields all day. In our villages, the 'fields' are patchy clearings that dot the thickly wooded hillsides far from our homes. Every household has plots here for growing vegetables and herbs. These are the open workplaces that their owners grow so accustomed to that they set off from home very early to work all morning, weeding, clearing and planting. They carry their food with them, and when the sun is high overhead they shelter in small thatch shacks and eat their midday meal and stretch out by the fire, sipping black tea. This outdoor life in the clear and silent space of the high valleys is addictive, and some villagers often spend the night in their solitary shacks. The others, who leave, pile all the days pickings of green chillies, pumpkins, yam and ginger into their baskets before setting off on the long trek back to their village.

It was on one such evening that Pinyar, walking home briskly, swinging her arms, had seen a young man running towards her at breakneck speed. He was shouting something, and sensing trouble she too had hurried forward. Then she had heard the word: 'Fire!' Hai! Her house had burned down.

It had started with smoke billowing out of the thatch, the young man told her, and then suddenly the bamboo had exploded like canon shots as the flames shot up and threatened to engulf the whole village with flying sparks. The villagers, the few who were around, had rallied to help, but it had been no use. Her poor-widow's house was gone.

When a house catches fire, the luckless owner is banished to the outskirts of the village. So Pinyar built herself a shack at the extreme edge of the forest. When I met her with Mona, she had just crossed the period of taboo during which no one could go and eat with her for fear of provoking the tiger spirit that causes fires and tempting it to follow them home. Pinyar was still angry. 'The fire swallowed everything with an evil appetite,' she told us, cracking another piece of wet cloth before putting it away to dry. 'It seems my destiny is cursed!'

She sat down with us and recounted again how she was on the threshold of a new life when her husband was shot through the head in the forest. But these things happened, she said. 'Every year at least three men die in hunting accidents in our parts.'

'Are all these deaths really accidents?' Mona wanted me to ask.

'There is never any doubt about these deaths.' Pinyar replied. She looked down at her hands and was silent for a while. Then she said, 'You know, I used to make this powder for the rice beer. I don't do it anymore.'

Then she told us why. Once upon a time, there lived a race of supernatural beings called the miti-mili. These small, quiet people were the first to make the mysterious si-ye that is the yeast used to ferment rice into beer. Before the miti-mili race disappeared, deranged by strange visions, they gave this sacred powder to mankind, and a strong belief grew that si-ye had special powers and that it was something to be handled with respect. Only women were allowed to handle it, and Pinyar herself made the best si-ye cakes. She mixed the white powder with ground rice and roots and berries and shaped it into small flat biscuits. 'However, they are strictly forbidden before a hunt or a journey,' she said. 'It makes men hallucinate, just like the miti-mili race. But sometimes some households forget to observe the rules, and then our men die in the forests.'

I was surprised. I knew it was very rare that a man who had shot someone during a hunt would be accused of murder. If he surrendered his gun and fled into the jungle to observe the prescribed taboos, everyone accepted that it was an accident. But I had never heard the explanation that Pinyar was now giving us, not even from Hoxo.

The man who made Pinyar a widow was now very old. Pinyar knew him well, she saw him in the village every day, but she did not hold him responsible for her misfortune. 'There is a bad spirit lurking in the si-ye that makes men go mad,' she said. 'That is why we sprinkle si-ye on the eyelids of those who die an unnatural death, so that their spirit will not return on some restless search.'

Mona and I were silent. Pinyar looked at us with her black slanting eyes and smiled. Despite her long, hard years she was lean and agile, and she had cropped her hair very short like a man's. She did, however, observe the traditional custom of wearing large cylindrical earrings that dragged her ears down, and she still wore all the beads, silver coins and amulets that she had first put on as a young bride.

The plight of the widow Pinyar made me wonder if a woman's heart is not bigger than a man's. How she came to lose her child, then her husband, and finally her home in the village was common knowledge. But there was another story that people did not like to remember or recount.

In a distant village, Pinyar's son from Orka had grown into an able-bodied young man. Kamur had done well for himself. He was a clerk in a government department that entitled him to live in a brick building in Pigo town, where he worked. He had married a good woman, a girl from our village, and was father to an infant daughter and two sons. One afternoon the young wife was in the kitchen. Her long hair hung loose, like a broad, thick rope, and she had a towel draped over her shoulders. In the adjoining room, her baby girl lay in a low cot that she could see through the door directly behind her. It was just at the moment when she had turned her back on the sleeping child when she heard a small sound, a sharp 'nyek!' She turned around and saw her husband standing by the cot, holding a bloodied dao.

Without a word she turned and leaped out through the kitchen door. He came after her.

The small garden gate was unlatched, but as she reached it she felt the blow on her back. She screamed and as people came running out of the houses on either side, her husband dropped the sword and fell to the ground blubbering and weeping. 'What happened? What happened!' he asked. 'What have I done!'

He was the one most aghast at the horror. He could not remember anything of the murder of his baby girl. And he could not remember how he had stalked and cut down his younger son who had been cycling in the backyard. Only the older boy, who was at school, had survived.

Kamur begged forgiveness. He rolled on the floor in agony and said he had no memory of those black moments. All he could plead was that he must have been under a spell. An evil spirit must have traded his soul for that terrible hour when he picked up the rusty dao and went hunting for his children and for his wife, whose loose hair appeared to have deflected the blow that would have finished her.

Everyone in the town who heard of the incident spat and remained silent. What was the meaning of this kind of thing? They understood that it was a nebulous zone that divided the worlds of spirits and men—in fact, at one time men and spirits had been brothers. They knew that what was real could well be an illusion, and that reality might only be the context that people gave to a moment. But they were shaken.

Looking back, they saw that there had been signs. At least two other men in that town before Kamur had acted strangely, and one of them had killed himself. People talked about the peculiar trees of the place. They remembered the aubergine plant that had grown to the size of a tree. Nobody could recall who had planted it or when. It bore small poisonous-looking flowers that grew into long, bloated fruit, menacing and shiny. It was a ghostly tree and no one dared to cut it down. Kamur had sometimes been seen under that tree at odd hours, doing nothing in particular.

As on so many other occasions, the community rallied to restore sense and order. Kamur had never exhibited the least sign of derangement or psychopathic behaviour before this. The poor man was more to be pitied than feared, some people argued.

'He is not to blame. It is something in the blood,' the village elders had said when we heard of the incident. 'There are men and women, guardians of history, who can identify this fault in the blood.' The old people of our village had sat around speculating on clan titles and origins, on births, loves, marriages, and spirits and ghosts. The right or wrong kind of marriage, the right or wrong kind of life, could always be traced to something in the blood, they said. Down the line certain traits appeared suddenly, in a nephew, an aunt or a great grandson. No one knew why.

'Some blood lines are almost taboo to mention,' they said. 'They see visions. They are visited by spirits, and like the miti-mili they are seized by bouts of madness.'

The widow Pinyar, I remember, was not part of these discussions. She had rushed to be by the side of her long lost son.

She wept when she saw him and she fought like a wild cat to shield him from the anger of the town. Kamur was put in chains and locked up by the local police, but Pinyar arrived like a whirlwind waving papers signed by political representatives who mattered. These papers approved a case for Kamur's release on the basis that his closest relatives would keep him, and, moreover, that no one, not even the injured wife's family, was asking for punishment. It was a long and complicated process but Pinyar's determination and swift action saved her boy.

'Come, we will go home,' she said to Kamur. 'We will go back to the village together.'

She returned with him to our village, and he lived there in his wife's house, surrounded and watched by her brothers and uncles. Everyone agreed that no one would ever really know what had happened. The truth, after all, exists only in portions, and the rest is a matter of words changed by each person's perception.

According to the account that I heard most often, Kamur had seen crowds of people pressing in on him. In panic and desperation he had hunted for his gun, overturning cupboards, pulling out clothes and running back and forth in the house. It was all a dream, for no one had heard him make a sound. But the sword he had used to cut his children down was real. He had found it on top of the big cupboard, in the depression that had been loosely covered with old newspapers and balls of string and other bits of junk.

After the madness, he had withdrawn into silence in prison, till Pinyar came to him. He heard her saying, 'Come, we will go home. We will go back to the village together...' and he broke down. He spoke in a stream then, like a frightened child.

'I know, mother, you think there is something wrong with me. But it is not true. I am only tired. This is the best place for me.' Then he laughed aloud. 'I have been sitting here all these years waiting for something to happen, waiting for my wife to yield with love, waiting for my sons to smile into my face, for my daughter to rush into my arms. Before that I waited for you and my father. Mother, I waited for you when I was sick and shivering with fear! Everyone is so busy, hah! Hah! My wife looks at me with hate now. Something has happened! She was so shy once, hiding behind that radiant hair. Something has happened! My son is afraid of me, as if I would hurt him. No one knows how this hurts me. My heart is gone away to that place where they beat me and beat me! Now everything has happened, and you want to remove me from this place where I have become a man!'

After she brought him back, Pinyar said, 'My boy is being haunted by an evil spirit because we failed to observe certain rites in the past. It was a mistake on the part of our parents and our parents' parents. It was my mistake too. But now I know what we have to do. All the great priests will come to exorcise the bad spirit. I have called them.'

In his wife's house, meanwhile, Kamur walked up and down, up and down. He jerked his knees, grimaced and laughed to himself. His heart was no longer where it used to be. Once there was a dwelling place. A place for safe return. Now it was twisted beyond recognition. Only one picture hung before his eyes like a drawing in blood. His ears hummed with the distant howling of children.

'Look what you have done! Look what you have done, you cursed offspring!'

'But it was not me,' he whimpered.

Sometimes his anger choked him and he screamed, 'I was a good child. What happened! What happened?'

This is what I heard. And all this, of course, is conjecture, even rumour. What I did see clearly was Pinyar sitting long legged on the veranda of her house, saying that she would fetch all the powerful priests from across the river to drive away the spirit that had taken possession of her son.

What is it about a mother's love, I wondered. After Orka took him away, Kamur had come to see Pinyar once, maybe twice. And it was only about a year that she had kept him with her before that. Yet, for years the fearless and outspoken Pinyar would break down and talk of the squirming, naked child who had wailed in her arms.

'When people looked at him he would hide his face against my shoulder. He was so shy!'

It was whispered now that Pinyar appeared distracted and that she was beginning to smile in a different sort of way. If I had asked her about her son, I was sure that she would have had all the words ready in her heart to absolve her boy of any sin. Kamur himself had never had a fit again. He now lived somewhere else and his wife had gone with him. Pinyar rarely heard from them. Their surviving son was already a stocky lad who had dropped out of school and was looking for a job. No one mentioned anything of the past.

The last time I saw Pinyar in her shack at the edge of the forest, she gave me an old necklace to carry for her daughter-in-law. I travelled so much, she said, I was sure to pass the town where her son lived. She opened the small package wrapped in cloth and showed me the old silver coins strung together with the tooth of a tiger and a wild boar. Symbols of luck and success, perhaps. Pinyar herself was not sure. She only knew that they were auspicious things to have. 'Faith is everything,' she said.

small histories recalled in the
season of rain

<<<<◉>>>>

In dreams, my people say, they see the rain mother sitting on the treetops, laughing in the mist.

Her silver ornaments clink as she rides the wind, brandishing her sword.

Every time she twirls her skirt, the storm clouds edged with black rush up to cover her.

'We're close to the season of floods,' I said to Mona. 'I should take you back to Gurdum.'

Every day I saw clouds dropping lower and lower like ominous waves. The hills were blue, their outline rimmed in black, and the trees were still. Soon, the first fat beads of water would tear the giant leaves of the wild yam. Then fierce, hissing rain would cover the land like the sea.

At such times it seems the heavens brush very close to the earth. The wild fruit born of this union is of unknown family, bittersweet, pungent, often misshapen and hardy, or swollen to an unnatural size. Hidden by mountains and covered by a charcoal sky the forest and rivers become battlefields ferocious with the struggle for survival. Astonishing plants with gills spring up in clumps. Delicate green shoots unfurl into monstrous fans and umbrellas with stinging hair. The wild berry covers itself with ants. Insects like miniature armadillos emerge out of nowhere and move about briskly until a flick of the broom transforms them into crumpled balls protected with green headlights.

It rains during the day, it rains all night. It can rain non-stop for sixty-two days at a time. Not a peep of sunshine. Not a breath of wind. Every summer the tangled undergrowth clinging to the hills is swept away by the downpour, causing landslides that cut off all communication and links.

'What is wrong with these hills?' the exasperated villagers ask.

'They're under a spell of diarrhoea!'

'What weather! What a godforsaken place!'

Mona, however, seemed quite content. 'It's strange, but I feel drawn to this place,' she said. 'Can't we stay longer?'

~

Perhaps it was the spirit of the place, I don't know, but every time I came back I noticed that the village had this quality of absorbing visitors into a forgotten newness of things. It was a feeling of how things might have been, and a sudden revelation of why it was not so anymore. This was particularly the case in the company of men like Hoxo.

But it wasn't as if change hadn't touched our land, or had come only recently. The first white priests, surveyors and soldiers had begun arriving in the region almost two hundred years ago, in the early 1800s. Since then, people from other worlds had come and gone, though the only records of their journeys are the stories that the older men and women remember.

It was already a confused and haunted time of change when Hoxo was found. He pointed to a corner of the house where the old basket in which his father had brought him home hung on the wall. It was a man's carrying basket, like a rucksack. It used to be the only thing a man took with him on any journey, and contained little more than a knife, a small parcel of salt and a piece of flint. This one, partially hidden by clothes and old swords, was smoke-blackened but still sturdy, and the original weave of the cane was polished with age but unbroken. I imagined Hoxo as a baby being carried through the forest in it. How could a baby fit in there? Had he slept all the way? Didn't he cry? Where had he come from?

'He fell from the sky,' Rakut's father used to say. People believed him because he was old, and because he had been with Hoxo's father in the lands from where the latter had returned with the boy on his back.

The villagers at that time had only a vague idea of the places the two men had been to. They knew that far in the east, where there were big caves in an evergreen forest, a road was being carved out of the mountainside. Reports reaching the villages said that the migluns were digging a tunnel right across the world. They wanted help in this work and a labour corps was being recruited from the various hill tribes.

'It was the duty of the village elders to persuade able-bodied men from our villages to join the work force,' Hoxo explained. 'The general feeling at the time was that the elders had been brainwashed by the migluns: What! Ask our own boys to go off into an unknown land and dig earth and die like worms? Everyone had heard the fearful stories of war. The migluns were fighting the Japans, and fires raged on earth and in the sky.'

It was said that there were different types of migluns, and that some of them had wings. Those from a big country called America shouted a lot and they were more frightening than the original migluns who were the Bee-ree-tiss. But when it came to building the great road for their armies to march against the enemy, they were one.

The men recruited from the hills were given rations and bedding but the work was the work of the devil. Those who went and returned said the forest and the skies were like nothing they had seen before. The migluns were terrifying in their energy and determination. In the lashing rain and the wet earth that buried men up to their waists they drove elephants to cross rivers, remove logs and trample the jungle. The elephants strained and quivered to the shouts of their mahouts, slipped, struggled, knelt, struggled on, and many of the poor animals lost their footing and hurtled off the mountainside bellowing like mythical beasts with their eyes rolled up skywards. It was unimaginable, what the migluns were trying to achieve. In the swampy valleys men died like flies, shivering with fever and fear. Sometimes, a miglun died too, wheezing and panting as he struggled like an animal possessed through the foetid mud.

Hoxo's father had initially opposed the recruitment and most people were on his side. Resentment had flared up against Rakut's father, who, as the local interpreter for the British sahibs, had been instructed that at least three men from his village be sent to work on the road. However, in the end both the men had gone off together to represent their village, which even at that time had fewer young men than women. They were gone for three years. When they returned, Rakut's father was wearing hunting boots and a camouflage outfit. The first thing he did on entering the village was to salute and smiling broadly, shout, 'A! B! C!' It was a happy day and the villagers turned out in a swarm to welcome them home. There was also great excitement about the baby in the basket, but Hoxo's father said nothing. When the villagers asked Rakut's father, he only said, 'It is a child. There was great noise and fire in the sky and then our son fell to earth.'

Even years later when those days were remembered, Rakut's father would talk animatedly of the thunder of cargo trucks and bulldozers, the shouts of men and how the jungle burst into flame as the mountain tops were blown off and the labour force struggled to claw their way through the rubble and drag the wretched road across the mutilated hills.

From what I had read in the library, I knew that this was the famous and mysterious Stillwell road that wound through Asia like a giant serpent, meandering more than a thousand miles across three countries. It started in Ledo in Assam, cut through our territory to the pass over the Patkoi hills into Myanmar, and then into the Chinese province of Yunan. The road followed the alignment of the ancient trails used by Marco Polo and Ghenghis Khan. It went up mountains, plunged into gorges and spanned ten rivers and hundreds of streams. No other road in the world had taken as high a toll of human lives as this one; it had been dubbed 'a-man-a-mile road'.

'You know, there is a wish-fulfilling stupa and a temple of the golden eye on this route,' I told Mona. I even began to wonder if I could not get her to organize a trek into these lands, just so I could tag along. The road was still there, I knew, and it was not very far from where we lived. One only had to cross the big river and drive for a day to reach it. The road would take us past the Lake of No Return, where so many airmen had lost their lives flying the 'Himalayan Hump' during the war. It would take us over remote and serene pine mountains to the teeming cities of prosperity all across Southeast Asia.

Hoxo, however, said that the road I was thinking about was now quite obsolete, it would take me nowhere. 'It is a forgotten path. There is only jungle and mosquitoes,' he said. 'There are no villages. It is a no man's land and the only people living there now are the men with guns.' He meant the terrorist camps and roving bands of insurgents who were reported to be using this route as a safe corridor between India and Myanmar. I wondered how he knew all this. But Hoxo was like that. He never offered anything conclusive, but suddenly, like he had done now, he made you realize that he was aware of everything and thinking deeply about what you had said.

I told Mona this. He was a mystery, I said, and sometimes I wished he would tell me things he knew and how he knew them. Where had he come from, for instance. Mona surprised me by saying, 'But why should you want to understand everything? Stranger things have happened in the world. Let it be.'

~

Jules arrived. He came in a hired jeep, marvelling at his own enterprise in having found this deep bowl of a place in the hills where a few lights glowed in the night like stray fireflies. It was in none of the maps he had consulted. But then, Jules knew his way around even in the jungles of the Amazon, from where he emerged with data to address conferences in the great cities of the West.

He had brought tents and canned food with him, and he whisked Mona away to a patch of hard-packed white sand by the river. The best way to enjoy nature was to become part of it, he said. So I spent a couple of evenings with them in their camp. The driftwood fire was a small point of light in the darkness. We could not see the river but we heard it like a familiar and permanent song echoing in our heads. It was cool and still. Jules uncorked his special wine and we ate pâté and cheese and vinegary olives out of a can.

'This is paradise,' Jules said. 'We should do this more often.'

Mona stretched out and glowed by the fire.

When we went into the village to meet Hoxo the following morning, Jules spoke about how important it was to work out grass-root strategies for forest management. He said he did not buy all the talk about innocent, guileless forest dwellers. He was concerned that we didn't value what we had and that our people seemed too eager to sell out everything to anyone who came with a little money and with designs to decimate our forests.

Hoxo then told us that once upon a time there had existed a green and virgin land under a gracious and just rule. The old chieftains received obeisance because they were akin to the gods. No one stole or killed and any man who could find his way into the compound of a chief's dwelling was automatically protected from all danger. In a dispute the chiefs would look up to the sky, consult the sacred fire, speak to the spirits and there would be justice. Food was sown, harvested, stored and dispensed fairly. It was a clan. Fathers and sons followed in the footsteps of their ancestors.

But the big trees were brought down. The spirits of our ancestors who dwelt in these high and secret places fell with the trees. They were homeless, and so they went away. And everything had changed since then. The canopy of shelter and tradition had fallen. The wind and the sun burned our faces. We saw a strange new glimmer in the distance. Our footsteps led us down unknown paths. We wanted more. Suddenly we knew more. There was more beyond our poor huts and cracked hearths where we once eased our dreams with murmured words and a good draft of home brew.

Hoxo was calm as he said this. He agreed with Jules about what was happening, but life, he said, had its own pace. Everything, good and bad, was inevitable. 'We need courage and faith in the face of change. That is all we can do.'

Jules shook his head. But he was thinking.

Out of the corner of my eye now, I saw Rakut making his way towards us. A crowd had gathered to meet Jules, as they always did to meet any newcomer. The village kids ran back and forth brandishing their catapults and making meaningless sounds just to attract attention. Rakut was walking up with his sideways gait and swinging one arm vigorously while the other was clasped stiffly to his side.

'Hmm, ahem!' he said, and pulled out a bottle of rum from under his arm. Then he said, 'Hello brother! Hello friend!' He said this to everyone, of course, and the women and widows and aging crones all laughed. Jules laughed too. He was relaxed and friendly. He shared the rum with Rakut and Hoxo and ate everything that was offered to him.

'I think Jules is a hit,' I said to Mona.

'Oh, him! He can get on with anyone. Send him anywhere and he'll be at home. He's like that,' she laughed, in love with him all over again.

The sun had set and all the stars were out, drawing anyone who would look up into dizzying thoughts of infinity and the permanence of things. Watching Hoxo and Rakut talking to Jules, I felt that they, too, would get on with anyone, no matter where in the world you put them. They were like that.

songs of the rhapsodist

On the velvet road they go
The red birds of summer circling the earth

travel the road

⫷⫸

I never made it to the wish-fulfilling stupa. Jules was in a hurry to get back to the city. And now that he was with her, so was Mona. Besides, there was much in our own group of villages that seemed to interest Jules greatly. He asked Hoxo and Rakut for places that he should visit.

Rakut said, 'There is one place you must take your friends to. The village where the migluns had gone.' He had an ancient kinship with the village, he added, and he could accompany us there.

The village where the migluns had gone. This, of course, was a figure of speech.

The early decades of the 20th century were times of great upheaval, when even our remote hills were opened up to the world. In 1911, a British political officer set out from the plains of Assam on a mission to explore the course of the river Siang flowing through the territory of the Adis. Noel Williamson was well known in the region, with twenty years of experience in dealing with the tribes in the hill tracts of the country. This time, however, his tour ended in tragedy. An angry Adi struck him down in the village of Komsing. Other men of his tribe joined him and then there was a massacre.

No one is quite sure what provoked the attack. Some recorded evidence suggests a communication gap: the tribe feared that Williamson would bring troops to destroy its villages. Another version says that the white sahib had insulted a man who later followed him to Komsing and killed him. There are also accounts that tell of a scandal some years before this attack—a story of seduction and romance between a local woman and another white man following the course of the river. He had made her reckless, and fearless like a hawk, and the tribe had meted out terrible punishment in retaliation. Perhaps it was the memory of this event that was the cause. Everything is conjecture.

What is certain is that besides Williamson and his friend, a tea-garden doctor named Dr Gregorson, forty-seven sepoys and coolies were also killed. Only three men survived to tell the tale.

News of the massacre sent shockwaves across colonial India and resulted in the punitive expedition of 1912, which became known as the Abor Expeditionary Field Force. It was a fearsome column that hacked its way through the chaos of virgin forest to capture the culprits and send them away to prison in the Andaman Islands. A memorial stone to Williamson was unveiled in Komsing, where it stands to this day overlooking the village longhouse. The villagers still look after the stone, just as the British had instructed.

It was an arduous climb to reach Komsing, Rakut said, and that the village headman, an old and pensive man, believed that maybe it was because of the massacre that they were still without a road.

On the day of the journey, the first rains pelted down and changed the landscape right before our eyes. We started out at the crack of dawn, driving through the mist and shadows and water. We passed Pigo town, through a terrific din of hard rain on tin roofs. We crossed rivers and streams. We crossed mountains of mud and slid across purple slush that made the car slip and slide frighteningly. When we reached the long bridge, Rakut signalled for us to alight. From here we would have to walk. We looked across at the dense canopy of trees and wondered where the path was that would lead us to the village.

Jules carried his camera wrapped in plastic and Rakut lugged our bags. He looked at my shoes and rubbed his hands together and laughed. It was not the best footwear for the hills, yes, but I said I would manage. I clung to the hard knots of cane as the bridge swayed wildly and threatened to overturn and spill us into the river. In my other hand I held up the green plantain leaf that Rakut had fashioned into umbrellas for Mona and me. This is the longest foot bridge across a river, and here, if you look down too long, you can feel the mighty Siang trying to pull you in by its very silence.

Rakut led the way and in the panting haze of rain-soaked clothes, streaming faces and trembling muscles we crossed the bridge and began the long trek uphill. Halfway up to the village gate we met a group of children marching back from school. They carried bright umbrellas and school books under their arms and watched us with interest. 'Hey!' Rakut shouted. 'Who is your teacher?' They said a name. 'Hah! I knew it. He's still around, is he, the old goat!' The children laughed and stood to one side pressed against the trees to let us pass.

There was an air of excitement as we reached the village. They had prepared the moshup, the village longhouse, for our rest. They had lit a big fire in anticipation of our stay and for the long night of stories, when myth and memory would be reborn in the song of the ponung dancers.

~

They have not slept for many nights. If they close their eyes for a minute, if their souls stray, if they miss a step, then the journey will be over before its time and they will return to the present overwhelmed with a sorrow that will haunt them to an early death. The man who leads them is dressed in a woman's ga-le and wears the dumling, an intricate hair ornament that swings with the rhythm of his chanting. He is the miri, the shaman and the rhapsodist.

Tonight, the dancers have arrived at the crucial point in the narration of their history where they will 'travel the road'.

A man, running through the forest.

He was following the narrow trail, running barefoot and bare bodied. Now and then he lurched to the right or the left, keeping to some hidden path that would take him to his destination faster. He crashed through the undergrowth and sped down a hill. Then he was running on flat land, then rising up again, and his breath was like that of a horse, whistling through his nostrils. This was all he could hear, his breath in his body like a hot wind that would suddenly fill every pore and vein to bursting and blow him away in an explosion of blood and bitter darkness.

He reached the village after midnight. The longhouse was ablaze with the hearths of every clan burning brightly. The faces of his kinsmen turned to him as he stood panting by the door.

'They have crossed the river!'

Now the women dancing the story move their hands in unison and clap softly.

'Where are they now?'

'They are camped by the ridge.'

Those other men who had crossed the river were officers and their soldiers. An enormous mountain blocked their view of the world. But they had to struggle ahead. They were armed with guns and they led a line of porters who carried food and weapons and helped the force hack its way deeper and deeper into the jungle.

Softly, softly, they must follow this terrible journey.

'Where are they now?'

'They have reached the Aing Alek.'

The force had reached the great forest of bamboo that surrounded the foot of the hill on which the village was perched.

A white man had been killed. A sahib who had come to the village bearing gifts. And now the soldiers were trampling the sad, disquieted hills and hunting the killer with all the might of the universe. Everyone knew it was the fault of the cowardly men who accompanied the officer. They had laughed in the face of the poor villager and said that he was a wild beast eaten up with disease who would never receive the attention or sympathy of the white officer. Why should anybody insult a man who was not looking for sympathy? Why should anybody look at a man with disgust when he was a man of the land and the other was a visitor trying to conquer the villages with lies and bags of gifts? Why should anybody who had spat on a man's face live? It was only a matter of time before the migluns learned that all men were not afraid of guns and loud voices.

All night the men in the longhouse stayed awake and waited.

All night, in the camp below, the officers planned and instructed their troops.

(One officer wrote in his notebook: 'The forest is like an animal. It breathes all around us and we never know when it will suddenly rise up like a green snake out of the decaying vegetation or descend on us like a mantle of bats reeking of blood and venom. The trees are enormous and sinister. They stand all around us and you can feel them looking down and waiting. One fears to move. The pile of rotting leaves and clumps of fern are hideous traps, and yesterday the stakes that fly out from there injured three of our native men. Their feet have been slashed open and they are screaming that they will die because these fire-hardened bamboo panjees are sharpened like blades and the points are dipped in poison. It is a terrible war and I wish I had never come to record such terror and suffering.')

It was not yet light when a long shout echoed off the escarpment. A sound like thunder roared over the soldiers' heads and a hail of stones and rocks crashed down on the bamboo grove from the village. The bamboos exploded in a burst of white dust as their stems cracked open and snapped into jagged splinters that could gut a man like a knife. The soldiers began scrambling up the rocky path. The stones slid under their feet and they grabbed desperately at roots and creepers.

The path was steep and treacherous, but the determined men were already halfway up to the village when the roosters turned their perplexed eyes towards a still invisible sun.

The sun had once cursed mankind: 'Every morning, when I rise, someone in the world will die.'

Now the dancers sway and moan.

When the soldiers marched into the village, the waiting

men rose and stepped out to meet them. It was bitterly cold. The men of the village were wrapped in their white homespun and emerged out of the mist like silent, sorrowing spectres.

They saw the weariness etched on each other's faces. Where had they come from, each wondered of the other.

(Before the assault on the hill, one young soldier had remembered that it was almost Christmas day. Across the ocean he heard the city of his birth tinkling with music and gazed at the lights arched above the shops from where people hurried home to fulfil the dreams of their children. It was snowing in his city. Here, the ice glistened like steel and flashed on the village from the tips of the mountains. Here, even the town across the river from where they had launched their boats was so far away. The jungle cloaked everything, the twisted ropes of creepers and giant trees entangled in insidious embrace. Sometimes they had needed dynamite to clear the way. What world was this, and why was he here?)

An officer spoke an order. A gun blazed into the sky behind him.

The dancers are still, and hold their breath. The stone ramparts are poised to fall in an avalanche of boulders.

Surrender is a kind of peace. The men of the village closed their eyes and recalled the symbols of peace: a broken arrow, a bent sword; the penitence of men who cut their bowstrings and threw down their spears to the ground.

When daylight disappeared the headman of the village called his people and they stood in a group before him. It was a sad instruction he had to tell them. Every day, from today, they would stand in line and pass stones forward, from one hand to another, until they had raised a tall cairn to the memory of the white sahib who had been killed. Soldiers pointed with guns and the villagers assembled every day to mark the exact spot where the incident had taken place on the slope above the longhouse. A stone tablet with letters was placed on the stones, and for the first time the villagers heard the cry of bugles as the strangers presented arms and honoured the dead.

The killing happened here, but the killers were from another village. But they were of our tribe. Yes, perhaps the white man was a good man; perhaps he would have been welcome in the village. But destiny was written long before he came to these hills, just as destiny was written for the man who struck the first blow. He was captured and taken away in chains to the island prison across the black waters.

Two men. Like an exchange of souls, one was surrounded by the brooding mountains, and the other by the restless sea.

It is almost dawn. And the dancers are still swaying to the words of the last invocation that claims all their attention:

In a house by the river a man and a woman awoke with the dawn breeze. Every day they had lain together and lived within old walls, shielded by the movement of big events that nurtured their strange love. Now time was running out, slipping away through their locked hands, escaping with the breath from their pressed lips and the light from their eyes.

The man had come to map the wilderness and trace the source of a river. He was a political agent on a survey mission, and all he had discovered was that the river was a woman and that his soul was now forever drowned in the jade heart of water.

What would come of this meeting? What exchange could be made? Lines would be traced on paper. A new picture would appear. Words would be written. A story would come to life in song and shining ink. But no one would ever know the other words, the secret whispers, tender, intense, spoken at first light.

The price of adultery was a bamboo stake through the heart. But the lovers had tasted everything already; the thrill of union, the pain of separation, and the unforgettable entanglement of the senses that was like a memory of dying.

The dancers sigh and wipe their eyes. The fire burns brightly and the shaman is a shadow man leaping up larger than life. He has sung of the beginning of the world; of the sword of five metals that ignited the bonfire of the villages. He has sung the story of his brother, the one who killed a man and became a martyr; the story of the hawk woman who defied a community to live in a house by the river. These are the stories, rhapsodies of time and destiny, that he must guard.

In the end, all we have is remembrance. The sword rattles and the dancers sing in chorus. They have travelled so far, like a line of devotees following the path of a sacred song across the ancient valley. It is a language that never ceases, and they sing because the hills are old, older than all sin and desolation and man's fascination with blood. The journey is almost over now. They are returning like a silent flight of birds. The shaman cries out. The beads in his hair glisten: the beads of the snakes; the beads of the woodpecker; the beads of the first man and woman. From the beginning of time, one by one the beads were crafted!

Later, the old headman said to us, 'They think we are a village of horror, but it is not true! The leaves of the orange trees glisten. The hills are radiant with the light of the sun. The laughing children tramp to school down the same steps of stony earth that the soldiers marched up. These days many visitors are finding their way here and you can hear their voices asking the way, the curious migluns shielding their eyes and asking for help to enter the maze of stories that the miri remembers and restores to life...We are not a village of shame.'

~

When it was time for the miri, the great shaman, to depart, the dancers put aside everything that they were doing and gathered to see him off. They had been together for so many days and nights, travelling the road, guarding memory, and some of the younger dancers wept to see him go. Before he left, the shaman showed Jules and Mona the beads in his hair and explained that these would be removed by his wife when he reached home. It is believed the beads of the dumling accompany every shaman in his travels during the long dance and protect him from a misstep and from faltering in the narration.

Before he left, the shaman chanted a last spiritual verse in honour of the visitors. 'So that they will understand our dance and why it is important to remember,' he said to me. We sat before him to listen.

In the beginning, there was only Keyum. Nothingness. It was neither darkness nor light, nor had it any colour, shape or movement. Keyum is the remote past, way beyond the reach of our senses. It is the place of ancient things from where no answer is received. Out of this place of great stillness, the first flicker of thought began to shine like a light in the soul of man. It became a shimmering trail, took shape and expanded and became the Pathway. Out of this nebulous zone, a spark was born that was the light of imagination. The spark grew into a shining stream that was the consciousness of man, and from this all the stories of the world and all its creatures came into being.

'We are not here without a purpose,' the shaman explained.

the heart of the insect

<<<<◦>>>>

Every winter, men from the surrounding villages perched on the highest ridges set out on a journey to the snow-mountains to harvest a precious root. This is the deadly aconitum that is collected for the preparation of poison arrows. No one remembers for how long this annual trek has been a ritual. But there are many stories associated with the excursion, most of them narrated with disbelief by the travellers themselves who say they were lucky to return alive, back from the realm of silent waste and hallucinations.

An old traveller, a rhapsodist himself, told us of one strange and difficult trek that he was part of. He would remember it, he said, for the rest of his life, but it was up to us to believe, or not, what he was about to recount.

The men departed in a ceremony of silence, stern-faced and swift, disappearing from territory that was fenced and consecrated, out through the protective arched village-gates covered with sacred leaves and arrows tipped with ginger. No one spoke as the chosen men travelled with all their senses alert, through the jungle of tall trees that shone ghostly white

'Our purpose is to fulfil our destiny. The life of a man
measured by his actions and his actions are good if their orig
is pure. From nothingness we have come to be born under th
stars, and almighty Donyi-polo, the sun and the moon, whose
light shines on all equally, is the invisible force that guides each
one of us. All life is light and shadow; we live and we die, and
the path of destiny is the quest for faith.'

Then the miri took the road out of Komsing under a sky
bristling with stars.

in the light of the bamboo flares. There were rivers hungry for lives, they knew, and mountains waiting to tear the breath out of their lungs. The piercing wind whistled and jeered around them, trying to steal their senses. The cooked rice that they carried turned to hard grain.

It was a terrifying journey, and finally they stood together on frozen ground and looked at the clumps of aconite that dotted the bleak landscape. They were in the territory of Dimitayang, the lonely spirit who stirs up the lake waters and clutches trespassing men in an embrace of ice.

Survival, as always, was a matter of courage and quick action. Blind and senseless with the cold they accomplished their task and faced the most dangerous part of their journey. Addressing the mountains and the air they turned in every direction and bid farewell with promises to visit again. They had to convince the jealous spirits circling them to permit them safe return.

'We will travel again to your beautiful land. Let us leave in peace now. Do not pine for us. Do not call us back. We will travel this way again bearing more gifts next time.'

Observing all the rules the men packed up and departed. The last man in line faced backwards and swept away their footprints to thwart any attempt of the spirits to follow them and come to dwell in the land of men.

How swiftly they travelled, never looking back. If the gods were kind, no harm would befall them. But danger awaited them this time. Like a bad dream a soft ball of dust spun gently after them, skimming the earth. Constantly changing shape the cloud gathered in speed and size and became a monstrous vision approaching fast to devour them. A strange light shadowed the land. The wind screamed. Dust stung their bodies and an unspeakable terror crossed their minds. Who could outrun the wind? Who would fight the air and battle with the mountains that circled them on every side?

With pounding hearts they broke into a run looking up towards the village gate. They scrambled wildly over boulders and leapt across the gaps shouting at the top of their voices. One of the men turned around. Greater than his fear was the anger boiling in his heart, and aiming his bow, calling on his ancestors, he shot into the spinning darkness. They ran, fell, tore off their packs and reached the gate. An eerie silence descended. Gasping, choking, they looked at one another and breathed deeply. Below them a soft cloud of dust-like smoke curled upwards and drifted slowly away. This time, this time the gods had saved them! Calling loudly and throwing rocks before them the people of the village descended to look for the single arrow.

It was a strange sight that no one understood. The shaft was unbroken and upright. Among the leaves and trampled fern a preying mantis was dead, pinned to the ground. The arrow had pierced the heart of the insect.

What did it mean? What spirit was this? For days, the men who had gone on the trek were like pale ghosts wandering about in a daze. Then the villagers called a shaman and performed the prescribed rituals to ward off the danger that had followed the men to their homes.

'It is better to call the spirits,' the old man told us to conclude his story. 'It is necessary to let the miri speak to them so that the territory of men is safe from their jealous rage.'

the case of the travelling vessel

⫷⫷⫷◈⫸⫸⫸

In this circle of hills, as in every corner of the world, all history is a history of connections. Suddenly, a day comes when a man will claim kinship with a distant clan, like Rakut, who had brought us to this village. He was not born here, and no one from his immediate family had ever lived here, yet he knew that he had an ancient bond with the village. He did not himself remember how it had been formed, or in which generation, through which group of his ancestors. 'This is how it has always been,' he said, and looked a little sad at not being able to satisfy Jules' curiosity. '*You* understand how it is,' he muttered to me.

At this point, the headman of Komsing came to his rescue. 'It happens like this,' he said. 'There are many stories that link clans. Sometimes we forget how these connections were made, but everything is interconnected. Sometimes a connection is born in the middle of war. Sometimes it is through a woman, sometimes land, and sometimes it is through an object out of the past.'

Then he told us a story about a travelling vessel.

It happened long ago. The Lotang family of the Migu clan

owned a fabulous vessel called a danki. It was made of the strongest metal alloy and it was an object of pride and admiration. Its wide, shallow surface was criss-crossed with fine intricate markings, like sword strokes, and a man could see his face reflected clearly on its polished surface. Where had it come from? No one knew for certain. It had been passed down from father to son for generations in the family. One day, the eldest son of the family noticed that the vessel was lying overturned in its usual place. He turned it over and was surprised to see it damp with moisture and with patches of moss on its surface. How could this have happened overnight when the danki had been kept under lock and key in its usual corner in the granary?

From this time he began to inspect the granary every morning and found the vessel always overturned and filled, now, with moist leaves and twigs. What surprised him most was that the leaves found in the danki were of a bamboo that did not grow in the vicinity at all, but came from the small, knotted, slow-growing variety of the hills far to the north of the village.

Being a superstitious man he began to leave the vessel outdoors. Every evening he wiped it clean and left it overturned with its face down. Every morning he found it face up, its shallow surface full of twigs, ferns and leaves. Word about the strange behaviour of the vessel began to spread. Many people came to visit the family and enquired about the strange phenomenon. But every time they went to the place where the danki was kept, it was found missing. It seemed that the vessel was teasing them, playing hide-and-seek. Till the son realized that the danki showed itself only to members of his clan.

At this time the Migu clan became prosperous and had many sons and daughters who married well, made a name for themselves and settled in far away places. And so the danki came to be cherished as an auspicious gift from the gods. When the owners held it up and tapped it, the vessel vibrated and tinkled like a bell and they came to associate this sound with their good fortune.

It was shortly after the earthquake some hundred-two hundred years ago that the Lotang family woke one morning to find that the famous vessel had split in two. The two broken halves of the danki had lost all their shine and turned a dull, iron grey, and each half was heavier than what the intact vessel had ever weighed.

The family soaked the two halves in the cleanest spring water, scrubbed and washed them with ash and the froth of the soap nut but nothing could bring back the old lustre. Immediately afterwards, people say, the two halves of the danki disappeared and the fortunes of the Migu clan began to decline. They became poor in sons. The last son bearing the Lotang title lived to the ripe age of ninety-eight. He had six daughters but no male heir.

So it was that after the disappearance of the danki the Migu clan decided to perform an elaborate family ritual that they claimed was long overdue. They felled the tallest tree and brought a hive of wild ants from the forest. The tree was a symbol of strength and the ants symbolized fertility and the birth of many sons. A famous miri was called from the mountains in the north but word reached them that he was away in a village close to the high passes. Since the rituals could not wait, the family called another shaman from a village two-days' journey to the east. He was a small, youngish man who did not impress anyone at first, but when he began to intone the prayers the women said his voice was delicate and sweet like honey. He stayed in the village for three days and during this time he was lodged in the Lotang house and accorded every attention and honour. As this miri communicated with the world of spirits, he must have succumbed to some misinterpretation or wayward instruction because when the time came to leave, he left the village with a bag full of stolen coins and a number of heavy necklaces of precious stone.

A maternal uncle of the Migu clan gave chase but the young shaman was fleet footed and there was not a trace of him on any of the routes that the vengeful uncle followed.

One day, on his long trek back, the uncle came upon two women quarrelling fiercely by a wide, gushing stream. He stopped, without wondering why he should have done that, for he knew neither of the women. But having failed in his quest, he was in no hurry to return to his village, and he hid behind a tree to listen.

'He said to share the beads!' the younger of the two women was shouting.

'Yes, so I have given you two!'

'But there were five necklaces!'

'I am keeping three.'

'How dare you! We should share the extra necklace!'

'Don't be so greedy. Two is enough for you. You're even lucky to get one.'

'But the miri said to divide it!'

'Hush! Don't make such a noise about it. Someone may find out!'

Now there was no doubt in the eavesdropper's mind that the women were discussing the stone beads. He drew his sword and rushing out of his hiding place killed them both without a moment's hesitation. Then he saw an old man perched on a rock staring at him. 'He has seen everything, I might as well finish him off too,' thought the uncle, and leapt on the old man and cut him down.

In the clear sunlight the uncle stood with his sword dripping blood into the stream. Three bodies lay among the boulders. The old man had swung backwards and fallen into the water and the women lay twisted and still a little distance away, as though they had slipped and gashed their heads on the hard stones.

'I came to catch a thief and now I am a murderer,' the uncle thought, but he felt no regret. He was an elderly man but still strong, and as he fled from the place, he felt like a forest creature that had done what had to be done out of sheer instinct. He disappeared from his ancestral village. It was many years later that the Migu clan discovered that he had reached the village of Sirum in the Duyang group, the home of Rakut's forefathers. He had married a woman there and had a son.

Emissaries were sent to call the uncle back to the village of his birth, and he returned, fourteen years after his disappearance from the place by the stream. Because the people of Sirum had taken him in, given him one of their daughters and revered him as a son-in-law, the Migu clan and all the clans of Sirum were now united for posterity in a bond of kinship.

'Such are the histories recorded by our shamans and rhapsodists,' the old headman of Komsing said. 'And in time of need, when a person falls ill or a fire starts suddenly, or when there is a murder or a fatal accident, all the remembered links of kinship are called up and word is sent to clan members to come to the aid of their brethren.'

farewell to jules and mona

<<<<0>>>>

All through the night the villagers sang songs and told us stories, and as more and more people crowded in to look at the visitors, sleep fled for ever. Jules was in good form and enjoying the endless stream of rice beer.

'This is the joy of living,' the thin and ancient village elders said, raising their bamboo tubes filled with rice beer. Jules nodded and Rakut chuckled with approval. 'A house is lucky if its women make good apong. Before apong was invented, you know, life was very dull. Men sat around feeling bored; they had nothing to talk about, they did not hold councils or tell stories or laugh!'

'And who invented the rice beer?' one of the women in the corner murmured challengingly and laughed. 'There is a story…' Rakut began, but thinking the better of it, took a long swig from his sloshing mug instead, making everyone laugh and talk all at once.

Now it was morning, and I heard the rain coming down in a hissing roar outside the longhouse. I was faint-hearted, dreading the return journey, the long bridge and the narrow, slippery road. When we were ready to set out, a village elder asked to accompany us till Pigo and both Jules and Rakut immediately agreed, though I wondered how we would all fit into the one vehicle once we had crossed the bridge.

But we clambered in somehow. I was trapped in the back with Mona and the village elder on either side of me, but this was good, because looking out made me nervous. The red clay had been churned to a slippery morass. A small stream trickling down the mountainside had turned into a torrent of brown mud. Here there was no growth of any kind, only jagged grey debris, as if a hill had collapsed and scattered itself.

'The river has risen, there is little of the road left. You won't be able to get across. All the labourers have gone and the bulldozer has left!' Voices of the few travellers we met lifted and were lost in the wind. I tried to jump out, thinking it would be safer to walk across this frightening field of rock and gravel.

'Get in!' the driver and the elder shouted at me. 'Stay inside, we can make it!'

And we did, in a furious churning and scraping of wheels in the slush and stones. Climbing out of the strange, sunken landscape, we spoke in muted whispers. Mona looked calm and Jules too was quiet. I felt my spirits lift. One hurdle over.

At the next water point we stopped to have our lunch. When we unpacked our leaf packets, there was nothing except mountain rice. 'What! They gave us only rice?' said Rakut. The weather had defeated and thwarted everyone; we had left the village at a run, with the rain pelting down and the sky crackling with thunder and lightning. No one had had time to think. 'What, only rice!' The village elder promptly pulled out a packet of dried fish from his pocket. 'Here,' he said to me. 'Let your friends try this.' He also brought out a packet of salt and dried chillies. We took our packets to a stony patch in the shade of a big tree. Two girls who had been washing a pile of empty bottles in the stream next to it hurried away, leaving their load, and watched us with amusement from a distance. The village elder too stood a little apart by the side of the road, as if to keep watch, though I suspected that he did this because he thought there would not be enough food to go around. 'I don't feel like eating just now,' he declined politely when Jules gestured and Rakut asked him to join us. We ate, standing in the rain, watched by the great mountains.

'Ahem,' the village elder coughed now, and placed a dried tree-rat before us. It was a great offering. Jules picked it up and turned it over and over, smiling and nodding to the man. The tree-rat is actually the red squirrel and a pair of these constitutes the traditional gift of betrothal in our hills. That is why most weddings take place in the winter months when the red squirrel can be easily trapped and its deep orange coat is at its glossiest. The moment the old man plonked the tree-rat down on the bonnet of the car, I felt some of my gloom and fear of the road and rocks disappearing. It was as if the land was speaking to me through this gesture of sharing: 'This is your land. Whatever happens, there is nothing to fear.'

When we had finished, the village elder came round to retrieve his salt and chilly powder. 'I'll take this, pity to waste it,' he said, carefully curling up the leaf into a pouch. Jules shared the last of his cigarettes, giving out seven sticks each to Rakut and the old man, which they accepted and put away in the inner pockets of their green woven jackets.

At the edge of Pigo, the village elder got off and walked away without ceremony and without a word into the cluster of tin-and-wood shops to our right. They have few words, these men of the remote villages. But I was secretly thrilled to see him striding proudly into the rain, puffing at one of the filter-tipped white sticks.

~

Soon the day came for Mona and Jules to leave. We went into Duyang from Gurdum to say goodbye. Everyone gathered around again, this time to give the visitors a great traditional send off with baskets of food and meat. Jules was wearing a woven half jacket and had a bag stuffed with notebooks and photos. Mona had wrapped herself in a bright shawl gifted by Hoxo's mother. And there they stood—laughing and taking pictures with the whole village.

Now that the visitors were leaving, I heard the group of women plucking up courage and whispering loudly amongst themselves, hoping they would be heard.

'Aiee! Aie, where did they meet each other? Are they Breetees migluns?'

I tried to explain as best as I could how the two were born in lands separated by a sea and half a continent, and how they had come together in an airport.

'What about their marriage? How do they celebrate their marriages?'

'What will you do with these things?' Rakut shouted at them. 'Will you write them down? It's the same everywhere. They shake the bed just like us!'

The women laughed. Rakut laughed. We all stood there nodding and laughing, enjoying ourselves. Then Jules pulled Mona by the hand and they both waved brightly, looking like they had absorbed some new joy in the clear sunlight which bathed my village that day.

'You who travel, may you not tire on the way!' shouted Hoxo and Losi.

'Hai, hai!' echoed the matchless Rakut.

And I felt happy for them, and for the village and all the men and women in it, for the elders and even the snotty-nosed kids who ran after the car hooting and howling like a pack of young wolves.

daughters of the village

We descend
From solitude and miracles

the words of women

◄◄◄◉►►►

A line of women moving up a steep slope. The pace is steady, slow. In the fading light no toil is visible, and they appear to climb smoothly towards the ridge-top flat and peaceful above them.

They have been in the forest all morning, cutting wood, cracking dry bamboo and piling stray branches seasoned by sun and rain into stacks to be carried back to the village. This is a daily necessity. The work is hard, but scouring the forest the women could at least stop, stretch, talk to each other. Now the unforgiving hill permits no speech. Every muscle, every trembling cell of the body is concentrated on the effort to tackle the gradient. One step after another they move, silent, with no other thought than to reach the top where they will tear the heavy baskets off their backs for a while and wait, bent and panting, for their bursting hearts to quieten, slowly, slowly, before tackling the last incline to the village gate.

Arsi thought she would never be able to lift her head again. Her shoulder muscles would remain fixed forever in a stoop, her hands clutching at the belt of cane bruising her head and strapping her down. She could not turn around; so tautly held were head, jawbone, ligaments, veins, that her neck might snap if she tried. She almost wept with the strain.

'Hai! Why? Why do we have to kill ourselves like this? Is this a life? Is this all there is? How can it be!'

A dry, stinging pain rose in her throat and spread to the roof of her mouth. Sweat dripped down her face and she felt she was losing her vision. But she would not stop, not yet, and rose blindly, climbing, forcing energy and will to obey out of long habit and practice.

The stony road led directly to Yabgo, the first of the hamlets of the Duyang group of villages clustered together in the middle of cane thickets and clumps of bamboo. Other meandering paths linked the older villages of Yelen, Sirum and the original village of Duyang. The villages ran into each other and only a tree, a rock or a narrow stream cutting across the path marked the loose boundaries. Great boulders lay everywhere. In between, one walked on gravel and dust. In the dry months this dust swivelled around and scattered itself in a fine powder that darkened the faces of the villagers and made them curse the place. The dry wind filled the chicken coops with dust and threw thorny twigs and insect wings into the feeding troughs.

Once, Arsi had tried to make a flower garden, but she had struck rock everywhere. Chicken feathers and some dry mud flew up as she struggled and scraped, trying different spots, but there was no soil and no moisture.

'Is this a place to live?' she had asked. 'Why did our forefathers choose this place? Surely we are outcasts dumped in this bone and knuckle part of the world!'

'What can one say to that!' Mamo Dumi had replied. 'This is our world.'

When it wasn't dry, it rained without end. The sky growled

and crackled. The days were soaked and the nights drenched. In this season when women split the bamboo, green snakes slid out into the kitchen fire. Where did they come from, the women would wonder. By what magic did the eggs hatch and the long, green adults grow within the hollow of the bamboo stem?

'Maybe it just happens, like in a dream,' Yayo said one evening.

'How can it? There must be a way, a reason,' Mimum chimed in. And at the end of a day of unrelenting rain, when the firewood burned badly and filled the kitchen with smoke, this was more than Arsi could bear. 'Reason! Reason! What reason?' she yelled. 'By what reason are we here with the rain and the mud and the fungus, can you tell me that?'

'Well, what to do? We're here and that's it. Where will we go?' Mimum said and narrowed her eyes. 'Besides, it's festival time, and we're not dying of unhappiness.'

'Who cares!' Arsi snapped. 'Of course we are unhappy. I am unhappy. Unhappy, unhappy, unhappy!'

She tapped the bamboo tongs on the floor with every word and then delivered a delicate thwack on the soft belly of the dog curled up near her.

'Out! Out! Look at him, he's the only one who's happy, sleeping all the time.'

The dog leaped up and looked at her with indignant eyes.

'Out, Botum, out!' she said now, laughing, and turned to me. 'What sort of place is this? You are lucky you went away. Why do you keep coming back?'

Then she said, 'In my next life I shall be born a bird.'

'And do what?' Mimum laughed.

'Oh, so many things. Sing, fly. Live properly, for instance. Speak English.'

Now old Me-me, who had been quiet all this while, said sharply, 'Hah! Listen to this bird! You should be careful. If a woman becomes too clever no one will marry her.'

Me-me had not changed in all the years I had known her. She had also said this when my late mother sent me to college.

'You waste your life thinking useless things,' she was telling Arsi now. 'What is the use? And where is the time to think, tell me. In this one life it is enough work just trying to keep body and soul together. You must marry. A woman's marriage beads and the obligations she fulfils as wife and mother are the true measure of her worth.'

Arsi snorted and smacked a piece of burning wood with the tongs, causing a small explosion of sparks in the hearth.

Once, she had thoughts of finishing school and joining college in the city. But this had ended when her father died. Now she said to me, 'I'll go away to Gurdum. Sirsiri knows a boy there who has a shop. She's spoken to my mother. I'll say yes. Sirsiri is a witch, but I've seen the boy. He'll do.'

~

While their men held court and negotiated interminable cases in daily meetings of the village council, the older women like Me-me sat in the sun and talked. They were bold, hard-working, forthright. They shot out words like angry arrows, straight to the point.

I remember the year I came back to live in the village after my mother died. It was an act of penance for having moved too far away from her. That year, I often sat with these women who had grown up with my mother, drawing comfort from their talk even when they spoke of sad things.

I remember Dumi.

'A woman's lot is a woman's lot!' she had said, and Yayo and Me-me had agreed: 'Hai! This is it!'

It was a still, muggy day in late summer. Sitting skinny legged on the veranda, Dumi laughed and spat. She had been ill for months. 'So how does one keep body and soul together?'

'Hah!' said Yayo.

'What to say! Who knows?' said Me-me.

We were all locked in our secret thoughts. It was a subject to tread lightly, especially with Dumi asking the question. Everyone knew things were not so good between husband and wife. Dumi the wise, the hard-working, the patient one, was fighting for her life.

'After all these years, when the children are grown, he decides to take another wife. Has he no shame?'

'They are like that,' Yayo said.

'It is almost time to die and he thinks about marrying again!' Dumi's heart was torn with rage. She screwed up her eyes and clasped her legs, gazing about her bitterly. The time to weep was gone.

'Day and night, day and night he sneaks around. After I bore him children, sons! And look! Oh sun! Oh moon! Look at this feeble man and see what he is doing!'

'Hush!' Yayo said, trying to shield her. 'Don't talk about it so much. Silence. Hush!'

'I call on you father sun! Brother sun! Mother and sister sun, let him be ruined! Fire on his head!'

The women stirred uneasily. It was a big thing to invoke the sun and moon. Words have magic, and powerful words have powerful magic. We knew, in these villages, that the men slept peacefully with no blame to touch them. The laws of birth, life and death were fixed and unchangeable. And despite everything women always prayed: 'Let no harm come to our men.'

The last blaze of summer brought rain. It rained like it would never stop. And when it stopped, the sun burned more brightly, as if to make up for lost time. Cicadas screamed. Huge green locusts thumped against the bamboo and perched on our belongings. Dumi cursed so hard her words seemed to poison the air and make us all fall ill.

At night, she lay rigid by the fire and stared unblinkingly at the insect wings and strands of dust dangling from the smoke-blackened bamboo poles of the roof. Her old bag hung from one of the poles. 'Give it to me,' she would say.

We would sit around her and not know what to say. When one of us gave her the net bag, she dug her bony hands into it and brought out her old tin. She fumbled with trembling fingers to break off a bit of opium from the tightly rolled wad. She carried it to her mouth and chewed on it slowly, pushing away all gestures of help with a hard, flat stare. A strange cry would escape her lips now and then, as if some glimmer of the true depth and expanse of life had passed before her eyes. Then she would sigh and hold her breath.

Dumi died that March. We kept the fires burning all night in the ritual wake for the dead, but there was no warmth.

'If life is not happy then what to do?' the women said.

Old man Pator, the oldest man in the village, came to mourn Dumi's passing. His bones cracked as he sat by her to weep.

'You should have gone with her,' one of the women cried.

'I am waiting to go with you!' the old man replied, blinking back his tears and laughing loudly.

Arsi, who was a little girl then, was squatting beside me, and she said, 'Why is life so sad when it is so short?'

The empty month rattled over the stony roads. An interior storm seemed to darken our houses, sucking away energy, hope, and dreams. In the evenings fireflies beamed out of corners and glowed silently around the jackfruit trees. It was a deceptive and deranging season. We carried water. We pounded grain. We gasped and died climbing up the steep hill carrying firewood. We trudged to the fields and smeared the young shoots of paddy with rice paste.

'Grant us blessings. Give us food. Oh! Great mother! Protect us!'

It seemed to me that for so little we prayed too long.

I chafed under the weight of daily routine. I decided it was a mistake to cling on to my past in a village I had outgrown years ago. I decided I should be practical; I should leave.

But the pull of the old stones would not ease. That was the year I decided to settle in Gurdum town. It was the best kind of compromise—half a day's journey by road from the village where my mother was buried; yet far enough to still hope for a life of my own.

a homecoming

><<<◦>>>>

We were sitting by the big window. My friend was saying, 'We may not have got everything we want, but we've learnt things. Life has taught us, hasn't it? Life is like an egg.'

It was a placid evening, pale and still. The hill closest to us was more grey than green and the stray bird we saw was listless in flight. I remember her wild hair, and the dark eyes frayed with fine lines and bruised with blue eye shadow. She was laughing and cursing.

'So what! Never mind. Destiny works both ways. Soon everything will be all right and we'll settle down to a happy ending, eh?'

We were meeting after twelve years, and in my mother's old house we were celebrating our reunion with wine and gossip. Whatever the years had given or taken away, on that evening we both felt as if nothing had changed. We were still two girls of the Duyang villages, standing at the same crossroads where we had parted once with such buoyant hope and daring. The intervening years had surprised us; we heard about each other's lives from a great distance and wondered at the roads we travelled. Now, sitting together, face to face, back where we began, we shared one single, stark fact that wiped away all our years apart. The men we had loved had not loved us back.

I, of course, had cut loose. I could not bear to give up the original image and I could not change myself. Somewhere, I would find sweetness and light again. I returned to my old home, to my widowed mother who hadn't been able to hold me back. She did not ask any questions, and I tried to show her, in few words and a determined stillness, that I was coping, I was all right. In fact, I had adjusted so well in just a month that my friend's visit was like an encroachment that upset my peace.

She had arrived unannounced in an overloaded jeep-taxi that deposited her half a kilometre from the village, since that was the end of the road. Young boys from the village had helped her carry all her bags and boxes to the house and she had grumbled about the lack of development in our parts and the money she'd had to give the louts. She flung her clothes about the room and kicked the enormous cardboard boxes to one side. I was struck by the amount of luggage she moved around with, and how she travelled alone in night buses and broken cars to reach strange, remote towns in her new avatar as travelling saleswoman. She flew to big cities, to Bangkok and Bombay, and booked single rooms out of travel brochures. She shopped eagerly and returned to quarrel with customs and bulldoze her way through walls of officials and middlemen. Once she had been beautiful. People saw this and retreated before her fierce face and taunting smile. Then she arrived in small towns like Pigo and Gurdum and the women succumbed to the new bright clothes, the delicate fabrics, the cosmetics and herbal remedies.

'It will make you glow,' she would say. And she seemed to grow light herself as she said this, sparkling once again as we did in our youth. Now, her body had expanded. She hid herself in baggy tracksuits and muttered in her sleep.

'The problem is we are too good,' she was saying. 'We take everything lying down. We love too much—but never mind, eh? You and I can't help it. We still have time to make money and live well. We just have to work and push our way through. So what, eh? Our happy days will surely come.'

'Don't talk to me about money,' I said. 'You know I am hopeless at business.'

'That you are! But you're lucky, you know. You have your mother. There's nothing like a mother in the end!' She sighed and shook her head.

Ah yes, my mother. She dreamt long, wounded dreams and recounted them to me on many mornings in a surprised, laughing voice. I knew she laughed because she was nervous. She often saw river waters gather around me. Once she saw me plunging off a cliff, plummeting down like a stone.

To be happy, a woman has to be born lucky. I was superstitious too. But I was not afraid. There were enough things to manage with, I thought. Books. Paintings. Writing. My mother, however, had changed her views. Years ago she had sent me to the town further downriver and then to distant cities to study, but now she said, 'Education is of no value. You gain so much knowledge and your mind goes off. What great insight are you looking for? It serves no purpose at all. Go out. Live!' At such times I pretended not to hear. I kept to myself and looked for words in the garden and the evening sky. Give me a little time and I will survive, I said to myself.

My friend said she didn't like the way I was hiding myself either. She herself fought in the open and was prepared to lose, but only after a good fight. 'So what, eh?' she cried. 'I earn good money and it is all mine. At least I can say and do what

I want, like all the men. My poor parents are dead but they were good people. I have nothing to be ashamed of.' Then she would add, laughing loudly, 'It's just that I'm a bit down at the moment.'

My mother enjoyed her presence. They had things in common. They believed there were auspicious people and inauspicious people in this world and that one must fight for one's place in it. They believed in conversation and food. The kitchen became a busy, bustling place, especially at night, and my mother was comforted by this. She had a terror of being alone and my life, so remote and unknown to her, caused her many moments of anxiety. My friend was like her in that too. She left the doors to her room wide open and grumbled loudly when she found mine shut. But I could not help myself. I clung to my private space. I groped around. Sometimes, when I thought I was safe, I confronted an image that took shape before me at any time of day or night and always without warning: two bodies, polished like mirrors by an early sun.

The man traces the lines of the woman's body. He weeps with jealous rage at a past that has known her before him. She vows to love him for ever. He tests her. He leaves, and returns. 'Write a story about us,' he said. 'Let us have a child.'

He left, and returned. The years slipped away. The sunlight became different. The landscape changed. The summers when they could move shadows and place them out of sight were gone. Love was not enough.

'You have to nag at them all the time,' my friend told me. 'Never let anything pass. Get to the bottom of things. Hang over his head like a harpy. Sooner or later you'll know. Don't weep. Claim, claim! You should have hung on just for the sake of making his life miserable, hah!'

I could not help laughing. She also bent her head and laughed uncontrollably.

'What about you?' I said. 'Tell me.'

'He lied to me,' she began straight away. 'He ate up my life. I worked hard. I worked for both of us and I prayed for a child but he had other alternatives. He is now living with a young thing somewhere. I have not spoken to him for a long time.'

'How long?'

'Since I found out and we fought and I hit him on the head.'

She started laughing again. I winced for the pain that suddenly touched my heart.

'What to do? My only right was to believe or disbelieve. I chose to believe. I made a mistake—so what, eh? I asked him point blank, and his look gave him away. That's the best way. Point blank. And then when I shouted—'It'll come to no good!'—he said, 'It may do me no good but it'll do me no harm.' I couldn't resist punching him then. We had a good tussle and after that I didn't care what he did.'

That year winter was long and cruel. Ghosts and spirits walked the riverbanks and watched jealously from the dwindling forests. They followed so closely it was impossible that someone should not succumb to their persistent presence. A young woman fell asleep resting on the warm stones by the river and woke only when the sun had already dipped behind the hills. In our parts, it is considered a grave error for a woman to linger by streams and rivers after sunset, for the night is restless with strange dreams and lost spirits. All of the next day, the woman complained of a heavy ache in her belly. Something had happened, and the old women who understood began to prepare for the rites of exorcism.

A shaman was called and the ceremony began with ritual chanting, calling the spirits to speak and disclose what they wanted. It was a bargain; a dialogue of exchange. 'We will slaughter chickens and prepare you delicious food. We will pour wine over the stones and scent the wind with blood and ginger. We will observe taboos and maintain our peace.'

My mother knew about these things. At such times one should raise hell, she said. People should gather together and make a big noise, otherwise your senses would be stolen. She kept her own vigil and we watched the great shaman murmuring and singing, entering the spirit world. Now, through him, the assembled relatives heard the cry of a young woman. Her sobbing was like the wind rasping down the gorge.

'I drowned in the green pool. My unborn baby died with me. I died there last summer. Oh help me! I want to live! I want my life back! I want to live!'

We are all haunted, I thought. Paths cross, stars collide, and even though we whirl away we continue to look back over our shoulders, for the debris of that unexpected collision still holds us in thrall. We all want our lives back.

I continued with my patient, preoccupied life. I was so engrossed with my thoughts that I barely noticed how the ducks were laying eggs again and how my mother watched them and waited for the chicks to hatch. A constant drizzle swathed the village in mist and often I saw her moving in the garden, planting and transplanting stems and shoots and bulbs.

'You'll get all wet,' I shouted sometimes.

'If I don't do it now it'll be too late,' she would reply archly and I would watch her wide shape bundled in her old skirt and familiar blouse drifting around the garden.

One day she told me her feet were feeling numb.

'How do you mean numb?'

'They feel cold and tingly,' she replied.

She had pushed them out of the sheet and I touched them

briefly. We had never been a demonstrative family. My heart beat uncomfortably at the unexpected proximity and I wondered what should be done. She seemed to sense my discomfort and said, 'Get the maid to fill the hot water bag. Then she can massage me a bit. I think that will help.'

I sat with her that night. I looked around the room and was shocked to see the old photos and how we had been smiling together. In one picture I, the only child, had my arms draped around both my father and mother and on my school blazer I sported my mother's old brooch. I left the room many times because I felt choked and ready to cry. The maid and she talked constantly for a while and when she fell asleep the maid signalled to me that my mother's breathing was very weak. I felt fear for the first time and stared at her. The maid placed her hand on my mother's breast and motioned for me to do the same. It was a strange sensation. Now I gazed at her face and saw how deeply the cheeks were lined and how the thin eyelids stretched with age. There was a small scratch just by the bridge of the nose, probably from a rose bush.

I dreamt about roses that night and did not know the exact moment when I lost my mother. She slipped away quietly in her sleep. I awoke to the terror of regret and panic like nothing I had experienced before. People poured in. People who knew and loved her, my old aunts, old Me-me and Yayo and Losi. They embraced me and told me what a wonderful woman she was. How she had fulfilled her obligations. How much she had loved and worried about me.

It is hard to describe pain. I had always coped by choosing silence and showing indifference. My friend's words came back to me now. You're lucky. You have your mother, she had said. There's no one like a mother. My poor mother! Though I knew that her concern for me was like a talisman that would never lose its magic, I had spurned it so often as an obstacle breaking my stride. I had shielded myself from her gaze with words and books that she had never understood nor read. Yet she had continued to regard me with patience and love. I remembered the stories of creation, of our village and our people that she had told me before I grew up to expect happiness far away from her. I remembered the quiet routine of the house and the fire lit in the evenings. I remembered her muffled cough at night. My cruelty stunned me now. What was I doing? Where had I been? When my aunt turned to me I broke down and wept. I touched my mother and clasped her for the first time in my life. I felt her soft, drooping cheeks and pressed her lifeless hands. I thought I would die.

'Come,' my aunt whispered. 'Let no tear touch her now.'

The ceremonial rituals passed as if in a dream. Songs of lamentation were sung, recalling the days of my mother's childhood. Her old friends sat by her and talked amongst themselves and to her. They asked her to remember the good times and said what a good homemaker she had been as the eldest daughter, as a wife and mother. 'There was always food in your house,' they told her. They reminded her that when the soul reaches that other place, ancestors step forward in greeting, and under the big tree the pure soul is crowned with a shower of sacred leaves.

My mother was buried with her head pointing west, so that when her soul rose, she would wake up to face the east and walk into the house of the sun.

The long vigil soothed me. There was great consolation in showing grief and sharing grief. My friend sat with me throughout. She did not bring any cartons with her this time. Life is like an egg, she had said. How unknown every moment was. Experience was not everything. After you had prepared yourself so carefully, life pulled out her greatest surprise and you had to start all over again. I begged my friend to stay. She looked after visitors and guests and walked with me in my mother's garden. The wind blew fiercely and wrapped itself round our bare ankles. My friend's hair lifted and she clutched at it wildly as we skirted the flowerbeds. Walking through the garden now was like walking through a minefield. Everywhere something had been planted. One could hardly move without drawing back in surprise. Sharp, green blades were shooting up everywhere. Frail twigs were suddenly full of growing eyes, and the roses, battered by the wind and the rain, were trailing higher and wider than ever.

Live, my mother had said. I knew she would always be with me, watching the hard, sad circle of hills and dreaming about moon babies. The earth was soft and porous. I saw that pushing everything aside the lilies were thrusting up with folded hands as if it would be a crime not to bloom when the earth was so fertile.

river woman

>>>•<<<

'Do you have any old family photographs?' Mona asked Losi. 'Any pictures of your father-in-law, or your own parents? Anything from the early days?'

Mona had become a friend of the Hoxo family. She came to the village every time she visited me in Gurdum, which was three or four times a year now.

'There is nothing like that,' Losi said to her, laughing. 'There are only stories that I hear all the time, and most of the time I think my husband just makes them up!'

But she went to a corner of the house and began pulling clothes and biscuit tins out of an old trunk. She struggled with the lid of one of the tins and rummaged through its contents. Then she came back holding out a creased postcard-sized sepia print.

In the picture was a young woman, with a handsome man in uniform. He was tilting slightly towards her and smiling into the camera. At once my friend and I recognized that here was a woman who was eternally young. She was radiant and dark-eyed and her long hair was pulled back in a simple knot. It was a picture of the legendary beauty Nenem, mother of Losi, better remembered as the woman who fell in love with a British officer.

I wondered who might have taken the photograph and how they might have posed, or dared to, in front of an officer's bungalow. She must have been very brave, Nenem, to accept the miglun's attention and give him love in return in the face of so much gossip and astonishment. Rakut remembered that his father, happily employed with the migluns at the time, riding the single bicycle in the village and delivering government mail, used to say that he had seen Nenem flitting in and out of the sahib's office many times, but that he had never accosted her. Only once he had nodded briefly to her but she had looked away quickly.

Those who had known her said Nenem was of quiet demeanour, but with an impulsive streak that was unpredictable. 'Like the river,' they said.

~

It was the time of war in all the world. Such a war had happened once before, but it had not brought many miglun soldiers to the Siang Valley. Now, they seemed to be everywhere, for they were fighting the Japans further to the east, where Hoxo's and Rakut's fathers had gone.

Of course, the white sahibs were not strangers in the region by then. Since the Abor expedition of 1912 after the Komsing incident, the whole of the Siang valley had been opened up for exploration and the numerous villages of the frontier hills had been brought under British administrative control. When gunfire set the villages ablaze, the elders had conceded defeat by waving tattered old newspapers. Some years before the war began, the British had set up permanent camp on the banks of the river at Pigo, having bargained with the villages of Duyang for land. The villagers had agreed on a square mile of territory to house buildings for the political agent, a doctor and a police officer.

Now the whole area had become a free trade zone with land and river convoys, officers, traders and porters moving in all directions. The villagers saw the lights of Pigo from their hilltops and were seized with a desire to learn new things, or at least to examine them and find out what it was all about. Everyone was flocking to this new destination which was now the recognized seat of power.

One day, a group of young girls from Duyang were walking to the market in Pigo. It was the season of oranges and the dark green trees were bursting with fruit. Every village in the area boasted the sweetest, biggest oranges, and the girls were carrying baskets laden with the fruit. If they could sell everything they would buy paraffin, molasses, maybe a wad of leaf tobacco. Or they would tuck the coins into their bodices and walk back home.

Suddenly they saw a cloud of dust swirling up and they all stopped.

'Aiee! It's the migluns!'

'Sshhh! Let them pass.'

They all looked down at their dusty feet, clutching their basket straps. An olive green jeep was driving up, and as it passed them it seemed to slow down. Nenem lifted her eyes and met the gaze of the young man who was driving. They stared at each other. Then the vehicle lurched and shot off towards the river. Yasam and Neyang started talking immediately.

'Aieee... I thought it was going to stop!'

'As if!'

'For what would it stop?'

'Maybe they would have bought our oranges!'

They walked steadily for another hour and a half, and when they reached Pigo they settled down under the big tree where other women from the outlying villages were already seated. Nenem chose her place and laid out her oranges in small, shiny mounds. She got her coin bag ready, the braided one that she had carried with her just for luck.

The market was laid out in a circular design, with wooden front shops that sold rice, cloth, beads, tobacco and salt. They were run by ayings, plainsmen, who all spoke the local tongue, and no one minded them coming and setting up business like this as long as they were friendly and gave in when the villagers bargained with them. In the centre of this circle stood the old, giant tree, its branches spreading out like a green umbrella over the tin roofs. A small paved path ran round the massive base of the tree, and it was here that the tribes occupying the banks of the river were allowed to sit and lay out what they had to offer. It was a jumble of food, vegetables, bamboo baskets, edible insects, jungle roots, herbs, ginger and local medicines. Some women even brought pieces of woven cloth and jungle twine, flapping the bright colours in the wind and crying out that they would last forever.

Nenem had sold two mounds of oranges when she became aware of a small commotion at the main entry to the market. She noticed that all around her people were sitting up and craning their necks. Then she caught a glimpse of a jeep and saw people moving out of the way as it slowly circled the market and came to a stop by the dusty little bakery. A man jumped out and she started.

Yasam poked her in the shoulder. 'Isn't that the miglun we saw just now?'

'It's him! It's him! Lets try to attract his attention and hope he buys all our oranges,' said Neyang.

'Don't be silly,' said Nenem, feeling hot and bothered by her friends' excitement.

'Why not? After all he saw how we had to carry this heavy stuff all the way here,' Neyang insisted. In fact, at this point she almost jumped up and waved to the man who, however, had his back to them just then.

People milled around. Someone came to ask Yasam about the mushrooms she was selling and Yasam spread her fingers and started counting. Everywhere voices were raised in the lively exchange of buying and selling. Some women with babies on their backs were standing up and rocking back and forth to lull the infants back to sleep, while shouting all the time at the older children for not counting out change as fast as they could.

'Hmm...Or-an-ge...Good?'

Nenem looked up. The young miglun was standing before her and pointing to the fruit. She nodded. He smiled and crouched down beside her. He picked up an orange and began turning it round and round in his hand, as if he had never seen one before.

'Taste it,' Nenem signalled with her hand, pointing to the orange and her own mouth. She watched him curiously as he began to peel it.

'Tell him to buy mine also!' Yasam whispered urgently, and catching his eye she began tapping her oranges.

The miglun laughed and started eating, nodding to express his satisfaction. Two other men stood by him. They wore khaki shorts, and belts with pistols. They are tribesmen from another country, Nenem thought, but their faces showed no expression and they seemed remote. The miglun said something to them and they ran back towards the vehicle.

'Where is your village?' he asked Nenem, gesturing with his hands towards the river and the hills.

She laughed and waved her arm in the direction of the hills. Hers was the village hidden by the trees and separated from this town by the stream with the iron bridge. It was the home of the Doying clans and was counted as one of the prettiest villages around because it was midway up a hill, sheltered from the winds that swirled and screamed down the river gorge. In summer it was cool and shaded by old jackfruit trees. But how was she to communicate all this to him?

'Aie... Ai...' Yasam and Neyang were muttering slyly and giggling.

'My name is D-a-v-i-d,' the man said, pointing to himself.

Nenem felt like covering her face with her hands. It was funny to hear a foreign name and she did not want to utter it, nor did she want to disclose hers.

The two guards returned with a large canvas bag and Yasam and Neyang quickly scooped up their oranges and piled them into the bag. In the excitement they might have lost count of the exact amount, but it hardly mattered now because the bodyguards placed a handful of bright coins before them. The miglun waited while Nenem put hers away into her small pouch. Then he picked up a small piece of ginger and looking at her mischievously he popped it into his pocket and left, followed by the guards hauling the bag full of oranges.

'Aiee! Why did he do that?' Neyang exclaimed.

Ginger was for protection. The wild ginger was a potent medicine against evil spirits. A piece of it was tied round the necks of young children to ward off illness and always carried, out of sheer habit, when a person was travelling.

'He must know our customs, then,' Neyang continued.

'These people, they know everything!'

Nenem barely heard her. She was thinking about the look he had thrown her when he dropped the ginger into his pocket. He was funny. Why had he done that? She also felt a little unnerved by the stir his visit had caused. Everyone in the market was looking their way. She had to pretend as if it was routine business, though she knew that it was unheard of for a British officer to walk into the market and start eating oranges with the tribeswomen.

Nenem was the only child of Sogong, the senior headman of the village of Yelen. She was nineteen years old at the time, but this is a guess, because in those days there were no official records of births and deaths. What can be confirmed is that she was one of the few women of the region to gain admission into a proper school.

A few years earlier, her father had taken it into his head to send her to the first mission school for girls that had opened in the town across the river. He wanted her to learn to read and write and become famous because he thought she was as capable of doing so as any son. For Nenem it had been an unimaginable prospect. From her happy days of intermittent attendance in the village school she was thrown into a cold, closed space and she hated it. She hated the text books and the prayer books, she hated the teachers with their flowery dresses and thin lips, and most of all she hated the room where all the girls slept in long rows like dead fish. After a year, she fell ill and would not recover. It was a great triumph for her when her father gave in and took her back home. She faced the mountains again and felt the river breeze as the ferry strained upstream, and was immediately restored.

All she wanted was freedom, she later told her friends. The

thing she had been most frightened of in school was that her soul might shrink, or be altered forever, and that she might never see the river again.

Now, walking back from the Pigo market, Nenem was reminded of the light hair and blue eyes of the matron at the mission school. The miglun's hair and eyes were the same colour. But in his eyes there was a smile, and a promise of something rash and tender.

That evening, the air was heavy with the thick, sweet scent of the sap of the jackfruit trees. Nenem prepared the evening meal humming all the time. Her father was sitting out on the veranda with the other men of the village, and her mother was poking the fire.

'Waah! What is this?' her father said when she brought out the rice beer along with small portions of chopped egg mixed with grated ginger. She laughed happily. 'I made it,' she said, handing out the mugs of brew and placing a packet of egg-ginger beside each one. This was one of the few days that her father was at home. Most other days Sogong would walk for miles into the forest tracking his mithuns sent out every morning to graze. Or simply fall by the wayside and drink all night with his friends. He was a well-known orator and had brokered peace among men and villages through the force of his words in many kebangs, but more than that, he was recognized far and wide as an honest man with a good heart. His only weakness was the drink.

'There he is, your father, look!' her mother would say, hissing with irritation, and sure enough, Nenem would see him draped in his white shawl, negotiating the stones of the village in a happy state of drunkenness.

'In the old days life was very hard,' he would say. 'We crept out of the rocks and called to each other because we were afraid to be alone in the wilderness. Now the ayings are taking our land and we have to creep back into the boulders and stones. Waah! But I can still feel my way through these stones. I know everyone of them, by shape, by size and feel,' and then he would actually bend down and pat them lovingly.

He was talking about the rocks and stones again, and Nenem knew that the men would be sitting up till cockcrow, whispering and consulting amongst themselves. Her mother had already wrapped herself up like a cocoon with the white homespun and was fast asleep in the corner. She sat for a while, appreciating the evening, her parents, her village, and all her friends and her own life that, at this moment, seemed to be brimming with an unaccountable feeling of happiness.

The green jeep began to appear regularly after that day. As if by accident the officer called David met her on the road, offered to drive her—an offer she always refused—and skirted the market place like a determined policeman in search of someone. Yasam and Neyang watched her closely.

'Hai, you better hide from him!' they said and laughed every time David appeared. 'What! Is he going to buy more oranges? How many oranges does he eat!'

But David was undeterred. He stalked and surrounded her and willed her attention. He had no fear and Nenem knew in her heart that this strange man was calling her into an unknown zone that could only bring disaster. What was more frightening was her own agitation when the familiar vehicle failed to appear, sometimes for days together. Then there he would be, suddenly, as if by magic, looking sunburned and full of joy to see her again. She felt drawn to him. For no reason that she could think of she felt as if she knew him, the kind of man he was. 'How can it be?' she asked herself in bewilderment, thinking how they couldn't even understand each other's language. David was doggedly trying to master her language, using local words with a funny accent that made her and Neyang and Yasam burst into giggles, but she, Nenem, had learned nothing and could not even understand the sounds of his!

One evening, after he had been gone a few days, she saw him down by the small new cinema hall, just walking past. Watching from the road above she wondered how she had begun to recognize his gait, and she rushed away, unnerved by her own feelings. She had no need to sell oranges or even visit the marketplace, she was the daughter of a revered village elder, she should go back. But she liked going to the market with her friends and she had no desire now to study or be married. She walked quickly along the road breathing in the evening air, feeling the sweat evaporating from her body as the wind began to blow. Then she heard the sound of a vehicle and knew it was him.

She was walking alone. He was driving beside her. He stopped and motioned for her to get in. When he saw her hesitate he made a sign that he would only drive her up to the bridge. She clambered in to the seat and nearly died when the jeep lurched and she was flung forward. He put out his hand to steady her and she held her breath. They whizzed past pedestrians and she caught a glimpse of startled faces. When they reached the bridge David got out and opened the door for her. Their bodies brushed against each other. He stood still and quiet and she turned uncertainly. He touched her hair very gently and placed a finger on her lips. Then he smiled, went round to the other side and drove away.

That summer the sun in the east narrowed the world into silent afternoons and long, slow burning nights. She had lost her fear of him and allowed him to walk a short distance with her. Sometimes he stood with her by the bridge. They continued to see each other like this, and six months passed. Small details captured their attention. One day she saw a green moon rising on the shoulder of the hill. The river shone silver and on the pale road they felt their souls turn, lifting and doubting, attentive and tortured. Many people saw them together like this.

From the sketchy accounts available of that time, captain David Ferguson was apparently an intelligence officer who had been recruited from the Bengal provinces to serve in the hills district and assist the new political officer in his duties. Everyone knew him as David sahib. He was about twenty-eight years old, an open and friendly man who spoke fluent Hindustani and seemed to have a knack for picking up languages because he was already quite conversant with many of the hill languages. He played volleyball with the police boys. Sometimes he stopped his jeep if he saw a group of village kids, and they would let out a great shout as he skittered into the field and let them examine the vehicle inside out.

He told Nenem, haltingly, struggling with the newly learned words, that his father had also been a frontiersman who had travelled widely in India and had even sailed up to this region in the days of the steamer ships of the East India Company. He told her that beyond the line of hills the river that they were looking at now curved in a great loop of water and thundered through a deep gorge that only a few of his countrymen had seen, because the gorge was always covered in clouds of mist and vapour. He made wide, arcing movements with his hands and Nenem listened and tried to understand every word.

It was an enigma how two strangers could be so unaccountably drawn to one another in a little town in the hills from where even the rest of the country was remote and unknown. With her very rudimentary knowledge of letters and books David might have been totally alien to Nenem, but deep within her she felt she understood his life. She sensed the big waves of the seas that he talked about, pointing to the river all the time. Through him she saw the world beyond. She saw cities and streets full of people and heard the skies reverberating with the sound of airplanes that filled her with a longing for far-off places.

In secret he too stared at her, amazed. Why was he so drawn to this quiet, strange woman who was young and unlettered, but who conveyed to him through all her gestures and expressions that feelings were the evidence of god within? He pondered this all the time. It was as if they had come together again from a previous life. When he was with her he smiled and tried to hold her interest, afraid that she might suddenly disappear. He explained everything about himself to her very carefully so that she would know him and not be afraid of him. But when he was alone he listened to the sound of the wide river and knew that it was he who was searching for the meaning of his life, and he sensed that through this woman he was beginning to unveil the secrets of the earth, the stillness of the sky, and even the depths of an unaccountable, ageless sorrow that he had always carried inside but from which, he now knew, there could be rebirth.

David's senior, the political officer, or migom, as the tribesmen fondly called him, lived in a bungalow fenced off from the road by a painted white wooden fence. David occupied a smaller bungalow near by that was shielded simply by a hedge of hibiscus. The houses of the migluns were made of wood, with corrugated tin roofs, and stood a foot above the ground on concrete pillars to be above snakes and leeches. Both the bungalows had windows overlooking the river. David brought Nenem here once so that she could see the view of the river that he saw all the time. She peered over the hedge and stared at the swirling green river. The sunlight danced and bounced off the undulating water and she felt as if she were moving in that current, destined to go... where?—who knew, but she was young and wild, and open to all influences, believing that whatever was happening to her now would have future value.

The longing for change came like a strong wind, echoing from the belly of the hills. It blew with such insistence that Nenem began to wonder if she would survive. It threw her into a panic and she questioned herself desperately: For what reason? And for whom? Why the longing to change everything, from the way she lived to the words she spoke to the thoughts that bound her? She was like a caged animal, crouched and listening to the voices of the wind, ready to sweep aside time and place when she became one with that fierce wind that called and sang louder and louder in her blood.

One day Nenem came down from the village with Yasam and Neyang and David was waiting by the bridge. The plan was for her two friends to go to the cinema hall then meet her here again so that they could return to the village together. Nenem got into the jeep and David started the engine. Hardly had they gone a short distance when they hit a cow. There was a heavy thud, the vehicle veered sharply and then, crunching hard on the gravel, veered back to the road. She had flung out her arm to clutch at him. He had grinned at her. The cow bellowed and cantered off. Nenem laughed in relief, and then he sped on, recklessly. A light drizzle covered the land and the mountains turned greener against the backdrop of the grey, lowering sky. He reached out for her hand. She did not pull away, and he changed gears with his hand over hers. They were both laughing now and when they whizzed past the last fenced house at the boundary of the town, Nenem did not protest.

The small rest house by the river was scruffy with peeling plaster and creaky wooden floors. It stood on a promontory jutting out over the river and was used by the sahibs on tour duty, or sometimes for a spot of fishing in the river, but for most of the time it was empty. A wild lemon tree shaded the house from the road and perfumed the air with its white blossoms.

The surprised caretaker rushed out to greet the sahib and called loudly for his son to come and carry in the baggage. When he saw Nenem he was seized with a bout of coughing, but he opened one of the two rooms with a great flourish of keys and said he would make tea. He was holding a candle stuck into the neck of an old bottle and shuffled to a drawer to pull out another stump of candle. He began to look around for a matchbox.

'Just light it with the one you are holding,' David said. 'We won't be needing anything else.'

When they were alone they only heard the rain and it drowned out all other sound. Nenem dropped down the mosquito net and laughed, seeing it for the first time. Then she piled it back on top again. David looked at her, her limbs moving and glowing in the dim light, and a rush of terror and desire seized him. When she said something he could not answer.

She looked at him and stopped speaking. He came up and sat on the bed beside her. The candle flame danced over his face and throat and she lowered her head so that he would not see her own agitation. A warm liquid was running through her body and she did not know when he grasped her hand. She tried to draw back, to say something to ease the tension, but she could not utter a word. She was drowsy, and his mouth was breathing against hers. She lifted her head and closed her eyes.

David trembled like a child, almost lifting her in the tightness of his embrace. She shared his trembling. He opened her mouth with his, probing mercilessly, trying to erase her hesitation, pushing her head back until she gasped.

'No, no...' he murmured, afraid he would lose her, and clutched her hands, bruising her.

Nenem had not expected this kind of love. She thrilled to the touch of this man who revealed himself so desperately. Who was he? Why had he become like this? His desire inflamed her.

His mouth tore away and slid down her throat. She felt his hands moving to touch her breasts and expose them. A deep flush suffused her and she arched against him, pressing the hardness of her nipples against his cupped palm. It was too late now. She tried to hide her face on his shoulder as he lay her down. She could not protest, she had no will. It was strange to her that he seemed just as helpless. Her wrap opened and fell away and her nakedness made him groan. Her damp hair swept against his mouth when he came up, and he held her down by the wrists as he entered her in an anguish of tenderness and flame. He wanted to be gentle with her, to take her slowly and feel the growing ache as he made her love him back, but she was turning and twisting her head wildly and whimpering. He grabbed her face and made her look at him. He sank into her as their gaze locked. He hurt her when he raised her up, tearing her flesh, punishing her, loving her, consuming her until she dropped her gaze and her face quivered and broke as she cried out his name and the tears came to her eyes.

Oh sweetness! Oh wild, wild beating! He raised himself and looked down at the whiteness of her skin, the sloping line of her belly, down to the dark mound where they were joined, and his body shuddered and surrendered. For a long time he lay unmoving, his head buried in her embrace. He was terrified by his feelings and wondered if it would be like this forever and he would never again be alone. He turned slightly to look at her again. She whispered something and clung to him. So they lay together, silent, for a long time.

In her father's house Nenem looked into the small mirror tacked to the wooden post. Her face was clear. The eyes looked back at her, wide and lustrous. Her mouth was innocent and unadorned though she could still feel the salt and bruising and how the blood had swelled her lips giving them the quality of some living, tactile river animal that moved and slipped and flowered with tentacles of fire. Her body had changed. She was complete and she felt no fear. She felt alive, full of power, and full of the desire to give and to receive.

When the scandal broke, Sogong, the headman, did not speak to his daughter. Instead he threatened to burn down the house of the miglun and drive him away from the land. He recalled that the Duyang clans had originally given the migluns a written agreement for only a square mile of territory to settle in Pigo. Now they were trying to rule all the villages. He would throw them out. He consulted with a few friends and they tried to help him with this unprecedented misfortune. A daughter of the village and a miglun! It was unthinkable! Yet they could not stop a woman from loving a man, everyone knew that, and Nenem was a difficult one. She was capable of doing anything if baited or prevented from doing what she wanted. Her mother cursed the day Nenem was born and cursed Sogong for being a drunkard, and in the end everyone ended up cursing each other so much that the cause of the uproar was even forgotten a little.

One day Rakut's father saw old Sogong rush into the office

of the migom wearing his red coat and carrying his long walking stick. The big sahib was a kind, elderly man with years of experience in dealing with the many tribes of the country. He spoke the local tongue and immediately called out to Sogong.

'Come, come in! Hey, Sogong, how are you? Let's have some tea, shall we?'

Rakut's father said that Sogong and the sahib sat together for a long time. He tried to hear what they were saying but the green curtain on the open door was short and flimsy and he was afraid that they might see him if he stood too close. All he could say was that when Sogong came out he looked very thoughtful. Perhaps the two men had discussed lives, loves, the way of the world—who knows? Both were aging men and fathers.

After that meeting Sogong did not say anything more about the whole business, though he began to avoid his own house, staying away for longer and longer periods in the homes of his many friends. Nobody liked to talk about the details and soon people went about their business and pretended to ignore the matter. Except the big sahib, who broached the subject with his junior one day.

'Captain David,' he said in his loud, clear voice. 'There is some talk going around, ahmm... about you, that you have taken up with a tribal woman.'

When David did not answer, he said, 'I am a man of peace. The people here are good people. I have nothing against love, or even love affairs, for heaven's sake, but don't you think your behaviour might jeopardize our mission?'

Still David didn't say anything.

Finally the old man said, 'You love her?'

'Yes.'

There was a silence. Then the sahib said, 'You're going to make an honest woman of her?'

'Yes, sir! I mean…But she won't have me like that. She won't come away with me if I leave this place, sir!'

'What, oh, I see. Hmm…' The senior man coughed and stared at the young man. His eyes softened. 'Well, they're strange here, these people. Yes, they won't transplant easily, I dare say. Well, be careful.'

After David left, the sahib sat at his desk for a long time. He tapped with his pencil on the papers lying in front of him. It seemed strange to him that so many years had gone so quickly. He had been serving in these hills since 1932 and the year was already 1943. There was a war raging back home and its effects were far reaching. Perhaps time was really running out now, he thought ruefully. How many survey missions had he led, to map terra incognita, and here he was now, at the end of a long career, wondering about the strange ways of young hearts! Oh god! It was time to be sailing back to England and here was another officer sailing off in the opposite direction on some daft mission of love. He was fond of the boy, but it was daft. He knew that David's posting orders were out and that the boy would have to leave soon, unless he could pull a hat trick.

Before a year was up word got around that the white sahibs would be leaving soon. All their friends and families across the rest of the country were already pulling out. The officer David would also be leaving before the big sahib. Yasam and Neyang were the first to talk about it to Nenem. They were surprised by her composure.

'Yes, I know,' she said. 'He will be leaving soon. Don't worry, I won't disappear! How can I go with him?'

Both Yasam and Neyang breathed easier now. They could

not imagine Nenem going away from the village. Many times they had discussed this and almost wept just thinking how they would never see each other again if David took her away. Yet they were all grown women now and knowing each other so well they were both aware that she was only taking refuge in a show of equanimity. But this was something that could not be discussed even among friends.

David left early one morning when a pale sky highlighted the clear line of the hills. Nenem had come to him when it was still dark. His vehicle had not returned yet from the fuel depot and they were alone in the house. She saw his face, silent and still. He was also waiting, uncertain, and his large hands were folded at his side, the knuckles pressed into the chair as though they were bearing all his weight. Love seemed such a difficult goal for them. She sensed his confusion and hid her eyes when he gazed back at her with pleading and devotion.

'Nenem! Nenem…' His words fell out like a cry, as if he was afraid that he might weaken, and she quickly rose and placed her hands on his face to stop him from speaking. He clasped her to him. She whispered incomprehensible words. He wept. She clutched him harder. She spoke slowly then, willing him to understand. She wanted to see him triumph and she wished him courage, she said. She wanted him to know that as long as she loved him, no harm would come to him, and that her love would follow him across the summit of the hills like a ribbon of light.

Then she had no more words to offer. The house was empty and silent, but for the men waiting just outside the door, scraping their feet, waiting to escort him to the ferry.

He left in a panic, a young officer clutching his canvas bag in the front seat and looking nowhere as the old jeep started and drove away.

Only when Nenem saw the small mushroom cloud of dust passing by the circular market did she realize she was heartbroken. She threw up her hands to her face and wept. 'Oh! he is gone! We will never see each other again! What will I do? What will I do!'

It is not clear if David and Nenem had really planned anything together for the future. Or what he said to her father before he left. By all accounts David had always been friendly with the old man, and had visited him many times when he needed to find out something about the place or the outlying villages, communicating with broken words and precise gestures.

The whole country was changing as it struggled to take over the reins of government from the British. New officers were arriving and as the big migom too would be leaving soon, all the headmen of the villages were busy with the constant arrivals and departures. In this period of change Nenem returned to her old life and quietly took over the household chores. Her mother shared her sorrow in silence. Her father's clumsy attempts at good humour touched her. He was drinking hard these days and the look in his eyes was old and tired. She wanted to say so many things but kindness shrank her soul and she tried to be inconspicuous instead. She pretended she was untouchable because she had overcome her fear of pain and hurt. She celebrated when her friend Neyang got married and one day gave birth to a baby boy. Yasam was also betrothed, and so life moved on. The war in the east had ended and Hoxo's and Rakut's fathers had also returned, full of stories of adventure and about how they had worked with the migluns to stop the Japanese armies from climbing over the hills and invading their villages. Men and women stretched their limbs by the fire and gossiped about their hopes and fears.

At night the sky above the village was full of stars, and every night Nenem said to herself, 'No one dies of love. I loved him, and now I am enough on my own.'

the scent of orange blossom

She stood with her hands steeped in blood. The legs of the pig stuck straight up and its entrails had spilled out of its belly onto the glistening mat of green leaves. A big fire leaped and crackled. The smell of roasting and burning wafted up from every house and mingled above her head in a dense fragrance of charcoal and wood ash. Everyone was talking at the top of their voices.

'Hai, here, here! Sit for a while. Have a drink!'

All the visitors were pressed upon to taste the rice beer in return for the gifts of more rice beer and strips of meat that they arrived with. It was the festival of solung. She delicately eased out the liver of the dead animal. It was still warm and slippery with dark blood, and she could feel the weight of it on her wrists as she heaved it into a shallow tin dish. Her husband, Kao, worked beside her silently, knowing exactly where to plunge the knife to extract exact portions of meat that would be distributed to all their friends. Now and then he lunged at the dogs. 'Shoo!' He hissed, and laughed, and Nenem knew he was happy by the way he worked: concentrated, deft, peaceful.

'That's a good-looking pig you've got there,' said Jebu, a young man for whom a chair had been brought out.

'Yah, he's okay,' Kao replied.

Jebu smiled at Nenem. 'Hah! Hah! Does he ever say anything more than three words?'

She smiled briefly. Making her husband laugh and talk was like trying to lift an enormous stone. Everyone joked about it.

'Hai! Look who's here!'

More people were arriving. Nenem rushed into the kitchen to give instructions. 'You can start serving,' she said, pointing to the wrapped packages of egg and crushed ginger. 'Tonight, tonight I will see everyone well fed and happy,' she thought. She ran out again and hitched up her ga-le tighter. The sweat glowed on her face. She felt the evening breeze touch her bare shoulders. She smiled happily when she caught Kao's glance. They were partners now. Step by step he had led her here— even she could not have explained how—to be his wife, and the mistress of this house that he had constructed with skill and determination over a period of six years. Perhaps it was the magic in a stone, a river, or a song. One could not be sure which.

She only knew that the beginning had been very different, and that though it now belonged to a distant past, the memory of it would trail her for ever like the scent of orange blossom.

~

For five years Nenem pined in secret. She walked in the sunlight and saw the budding life hidden in the cold winter stems and shrubs. One morning the peach trees opened in pale pink blossoms, and eleven ducklings hatched with yellow breasts and bills, identical to their mother's. They tottered and crept under her wing. The drake looked fierce and stared around hissing and breathing hard though he kept ducking his head to the mother duck as if in perplexed obeisance. Then the mother rose and left the straggling chicks and nipped hard at him. He darted away, while she calmly waddled into the garden shaking her feathers, shaking off the long wait of gestation, dipped her head into the tin trough and began to splash and clean herself. Then she swept into the undergrowth in great excitement and the chicks ran up to her as fast as they could.

The green of living! The young shoots of plants, the sun and dew. The living mud, the stirring of worms. Nenem smiled to see the duck's great hunger and rejoiced in her performance and release.

It was during this time, maybe three or four years after David had left, that she received a tattered envelope marked with blue lines and covered with colourful postage. Rakut's father had brought it to her and though he tried to look very casual Nenem knew he was dying of curiosity. He said, 'Here, it must have been held up somewhere. I brought it as soon as I saw it. I've also signed for it in the delivery register.'

She was touched by his concern. He continued, 'By the way, I hear a new band of musicians is going to play something in the town hall tonight. You should come and see it.'

'Okay.' Nenem gave in because he had brought the letter, and because the fellow was like her own brother, after all. He had never made any comment to her or to anyone else about the times when he had seen her visiting David's house. And now here he was, back from the wars and tinkling his cycle bell as though he had never been away, and still silent about both her recklessness and her misfortune.

When she opened the envelope she saw the photograph. There was nothing else, but there was no need of anything else. The years fell away and she saw herself again, so innocent and happy! She stared and stared at the picture.

She saw David. Yes, there he was, tilting towards her with that expression on his face, but she was trying to see more—the house in the background, the reflection of a windowpane, the tip of the hibiscus bush, and the colour of the sky. At the back David had written his name and put a thumbprint over it. She smiled, remembering everything about him. He was so funny! She remembered the colour of his eyes, like the sky seen in the river, and the weight of his hand on hers, driving that old jeep and grinning happily at her while the whole world was moving and changing. Everything came back in a rush until she couldn't see anymore because her eyes were full of tears.

That evening Nenem took great pains to appear fresh and beautiful. She scrubbed her face until it glowed. She pinned back her hair with a new clip and searched for clothes that would brighten her appearance. In a last-minute decision she put on her green beads and carried her small coin purse.

The small town hall was packed; in just a couple of years Pigo had become twice its old size. She regretted that she had not sought out Rakut's father to escort her, but then, maybe he had just invited her because he felt sorry for her, thinking that she would not come. She was about to turn away when a quiet voice greeted her. It was a man she had never seen before. 'Oh...' she said, hesitating. Just then Rakut's father dashed up smiling and greeted them both. 'This is Kao,' he said, almost pushing Nenem against the young man who, however, did not smile. Instead he stood silently and looked around as if he was embarrassed by the introduction. Then a loud voice announced that the cultural show was about to begin and everyone should sit down immediately and those people standing at the back should either leave or remain silent! Rakut's father was one of the members of the organizing committee and he rushed away, but not before telling them excitedly that this show was 'all about preserving our roots', because already the past was being cast away by many young people.

Kao screwed up his face at the noise and harsh lights. The announcer shouted, the tall microphone before him screeched and the sound box crackled and hissed through the two loudspeakers on either side of the stage that Nenem was seeing for the first time. She had never heard such sounds before. The stage was decorated with tall stems of freshly cut bamboo, and on the backdrop was a cloth banner with big, bold letters in the miglun language that Nenem could barely decipher: W-E-L-C-O-M-E

Two women came out and stood quietly on stage. Nenem stared at them. They were dressed in short black skirts and covered in beads. She realized they were women from distant villages across the river. How times had changed! People were moving freely across the region and new settlers from the outlying villages were pouring into the town. Now the women swayed slightly and held their hands behind their backs as if they were uncertain where or how to begin. There were no instruments and no extra accompaniments. They did not look at one another but they started together on cue as if someone was signalling to them. Their song began softly, and as Nenem strained to make out the words, it became a rising sound, a soft moaning wind sweeping across the land. One voice rose, the other sighed and the notes fell like waves. It was a vaguely familiar sound, it reminded her of something deep and distant even though it was in a tongue she could not understand, for the women singing were from a faraway place. But the song was so clear, so pure and melodious that to anyone who heard it the thought was sure to cross their minds that this was of no known language and that it was never spoken but always sung, like this.

The two women were communicating like songbirds. It must be a lament, Nenem thought, and imagined a bird flying high in the sky bringing news of death while the wind caught the soft feathers slowly spiralling earthwards. The song rose, echoed, and wept without any visible change of expression on the faces of the singers except once, when in the long exchange of notes she saw the smile growing in their eyes as they took the notes higher and higher like dancing leaves that soared skywards until they disappeared. The audience was left breathless. It was an impossible music. Nenem felt her throat choked with tears. What were they singing about?

She looked quickly at Kao. He appeared imperturbable in his seat but he clapped and now looked at her as if to say, 'Well, what about this, huh?' And for some reason, looking at him, at the way he tilted his head towards her slightly, she understood why the song had seemed familiar. It was about loss, the kind that she had known when the man she had loved went away. It was the kind of loss she had understood long before she suffered it, listening as a little girl to an old ballad sung by the villagers to bless their warrior sons. Perhaps these women had been singing similar words:

These were our arrows,
This, our poison.
This, the warrior's art,
These, our songs of love.

This was her land. She had chosen it over love. She did not ask herself if she was happy.

It was another summer. Clouds would swoop down over the hills, threatening rain, and then suddenly surrender, leaving the evening sky filled with a strange, wild glow. Kao came to visit her often. He came to Yelen from the village of Motum across the river to board the big ferry that took him further downstream to the distant town where he was completing his studies. He was the eldest son of the Poro family and was one of the first men of the area to be travelling out so far. Everyone spoke of him with affection and praise. Kao, however, never said much at all. This silence provoked Nenem, who began to talk and open up just so that she could tease him and extract a few words from him. How could she have known that the serious Kao was enchanted by her gossip, her trusting face, her lips, her eyes, and that he longed for the heat and musk of her woman's body?

It took a long time for him to break his silence. Nenem was shocked by his proposal and when he came again to speak to her father she hid herself by the granary buildings at the outskirts of the village. She saw that the clouds had drifted down low during the night, and without the sun they were cradled in the mountains and still clinging to the trees.

'There are so many things to share,' she thought wistfully.

'Yes, yes,' her old aunt had also told her when David had gone away. 'Let him go. Don't hurt yourself. You will see, there are so many other good people in the world. Give your love, share your life and make someone happy. These are enough gifts for one lifetime. Don't sacrifice your life for a dream!'

Oh! How long ago that seemed now. David! She would never forget him. As long as there was life and breath in her body he would be there with her. She had promised herself that. Yet her heart was beating wildly wondering what Kao and her father would be discussing. She knew intuitively that Kao would be a good husband.

'Ah, what will happen?' she asked herself, realizing now that the true sadness of love is the old, undying image being slowly replaced by the expectation of a new love.

Nenem and Kao became man and wife amidst great joy and celebration. Rakut's father was the one who worked day and night to see that everything was done according to custom. Old men and women whom no one had ever seen before arrived from villages no one had heard of, and the slaughter of mithuns and the consumption of food and drink was something that no one could ever forget. The ceremony was especially distinguished by the presence of Hoxo's father, Lutor, who had come to wish the family. Old Sogong and his wife sat on the veranda and shouted and joked in great excitement, for they were relieved and happy for their daughter. She was going to a good home—Kao's family had brought rich gifts of mithuns and old metal plates and dishes. There was even a road that the British had built which passed right at the edge of the village. Only one other village in all their hills had a road close to it.

The marriage was also the cementing of wider ties with villages on the other side of the river, between the powerful Doying and Poro clans, and this was an important alliance for the kebang abus, the village elders, who would be travelling there on many future missions to resolve cases with their powers of oratory.

Nenem's childhood friends Yasam and Neyang wept when they came down to the ferry ghat. They were carrying enormous bundles and an old tin trunk that contained everything that Nenem would need to begin her new life in Motum.

'Yes,' Nenem said to herself, 'tonight I will see everyone well fed and happy!'

It was the festival of solung and the celebration of her first year of marriage. The conversation was loud and lively. Everyone had something to say. Old aches and pains were disclosed.

Personal preferences revealed. In one corner some women spoke in hushed tones then burst into loud peals of laughter. The fire seemed to turn and twist as if trying to light up all the faces. A breeze gathered force and carried with it the scent of rain. Jebu said everyone should sing. No sooner had he said this than the company heard the rumbling entry of a lorry that had been hired to transport the ponung girls from the neighbouring villages who were going to sing and dance all night.

'Whatever one may say, we all become like the ones before us,' said Kinu. Then he turned to the women huddled in the corner and said, 'Now you ladies there—don't be so serious! Get ready to sing and drink!'

'When you get to be like us you will also grow serious,' retorted the oldest one of the group. 'You just wait and see. But we will sing, of course! Why not?'

'Hai, whatever one may say everyone of us follows in the footsteps of the ones before us!' Kinu kept repeating to himself.

The girls spilled out of the lorry, already making music with their long necklaces of silver coins. They were dressed in identical red ga-les with short black jackets. There were twenty girls in all and they looked fresh and eager, each one nudging her friend as they shuffled towards the fire.

'What beauties! Hai, the young girls are here!' shouted Kinu.

The girls giggled.

'Everyone must sing!' Kinu shouted again, and almost spilling his drink he rushed across to Kao and began hauling him up. Kao was smiling and shaking his head. Then he washed his hands in the bucket of water and stood up. Nenem watched him closely and heard him clearing his throat. Everyone laughed and clapped. They laughed more when Kao started singing a very slow, serious song.

'Hai! Hai! Stop him someone, this won't do!' shouted Kinu.

There was great merriment while Kao continued to sing with his hands in his pocket. Nenem laughed and they looked at each other, Kao still grinning and singing, until Kinu cried out loudly that Kao should be exempted immediately or he would spoil the evening with his pitiful sobriety.

Nenem looked up at the sky. The moon sailed brightly on a ragged black veil and a looming pillar of cloud began to cover half the sky. It seemed to her that heaven itself was sloping downwards in a shaft of light and it gave her a thrill to feel the evening deepening. This was her world now. A small village in the wilderness, the big clouds moving overhead and the faces of her family and friends shining in the firelight. Yes, a moment of happiness like this! She breathed in deeply, and felt the baby kicking in her womb.

'The rains are not over yet,' Kao had told her the other night when she had cried out about her flowers and seeds. Kao had staked the earth for her scented creepers and she was impatient for rain. 'Wait a bit,' he had said, and sure enough, the downpour had come one night hissing and splashing. Nenem had conceded defeat. Now she smiled, remembering this careful and attentive trait of Kao's. A row of budding cassia trees in a straight row was his handiwork, and he had helped her plant her orange trees in a sheltered grove on the slope of the hill that overlooked the river.

We remember things by little signposts that we have planted here and there, she thought. She had planted the orange trees thinking that she would never escape the scent of orange blossom. And now when she looked at the trees she recalled all the fragments of the past that no one but she could understand. Time had changed so many things.

Nothing was complete. But there was comfort in looking at the green hills and the river that she had crossed to become Kao's wife. Together, they would raise a family, guard their land and live among their people observing the ancient customs of their clan. Surely these were enough gifts for one lifetime.

rites of love

❮❮❮◆❯❯❯

Of all the stories I had heard from Hoxo, I could sense that he brought the most affection and imagination to incidents that concerned Nenem. To him she was like the river, constant, nurturing, self-possessed. Like the river, she was the soul of our land. He had never seen Nenem, only imagined her through the free spirit, good sense and warm eyes of her daughter Losi, who became his wife. It was fire that brought them together.

In the old days, fire watching had been a sacred duty. All young men were expected to give their time, taking turns to stay together in the bango, the boys' dormitory, and keep vigil through the night. The old men and women took up this duty during the day, when they also minded the young children while their parents were away in the fields. One night, a terrible fire broke out in Motum village. The people of Duyang were aroused by the sound of explosions. Running up to the highest point and looking across the river in the darkness they saw what appeared to be an island of fire dancing and sliding on the treetops. 'It's a fire!' they shouted. They could almost hear the screams of men and animals and they stood for a long time shouting into the wind and calling on the gods to save the poor villagers.

Twenty houses were completely gutted, one house leaping like a ball of flame on to the other until the villagers had moved boulders and trees with superhuman strength to erect a barricade against the angry fire spirit. The village had to perform special rituals to cleanse itself of the tragedy, and like in all other villages, clansmen from far away, on hearing the news, had hurried to help rebuild the destroyed houses. The new dwellings were ready within a week and except for the charred branches of some old trees a visitor to the place would not have seen any trace of the devastation.

It was at this time that Hoxo had volunteered to join a band of youth who were setting out to keep the fire vigil in Motum village. This was a gesture of solidarity, and since Rakut was also going, the two friends made their first journey across the river together. The village of Motum was perched high on a plateau that overlooked the surrounding hills. Here, the land opened out into wide, rolling slopes while even taller mountains glistening with snow girdled the village itself. These were the mountains where the wild aconite grew.

Hoxo recalled that this had been one of his happiest times. Every night the boys gathered in the bango and lolled around the fire. Sometimes, in a fit of exuberance, they would march though the village swinging the hurricane lamp and calling, 'Watch your fires! Watch! Watch! Everybody, watch your fires!'

One unforgettable night Hoxo and Rakut rushed into a house thinking the fire was burning too brightly for such a late hour. Because they had panicked—the memory of the great fire was still fresh in their minds—they did not call out or ask permission to enter. They leaped up onto the bamboo platform and peered in. Hoxo saw a young girl holding aloft what looked like a book, under a pole from which was hung a hurricane lamp, just like the one he was carrying. Someone grunted from the corner and the girl immediately dropped the book with a thud.

'What! Who's there?'

Hoxo realized he was in the house of Kao and felt his face burning. What with all the new houses in the village they had failed to recognize the famous house of Nenem and Kao. This must be their daughter!

'It's the way things happen,' Hoxo reminded me, laughing. He would not say any more but everyone knew the story— Hoxo and Rakut had mumbled something, and Kao had invited them in, since they had woken him up. But Losi, the daughter, had made no attempt to conceal her displeasure at their rude intrusion.

Losi had had a solitary childhood. She grew up in a house that was built in the traditional style with a projecting bamboo veranda perched on stilts. A unique extension to the house was a long room made of solid wood that Kao had designed for Nenem. The room even contained some wicker chairs, and a tin trunk draped with cloth had been turned into another seat. This trunk was a treasure trove that Losi often explored avidly, and the book she had been staring at in the light of the hurricane lamp had come out of this.

'Keep this, this is the box of stories,' her mother had told her. 'You can shape them, colour them, and pull them out anytime.' She had showed the child Losi the small box with the pink jade lid that smelled sweet and comforting, and had held up the big copper-coloured binoculars for her to peer through. This was a gift that David had left for Nenem's father. It was stamped: 1902, and for a long time it had hung on the high rafters along with the firewood and other household paraphernalia because Nenem had been too shy to touch it and

Sogong, perhaps, too angry. It must have been her mother who had finally wrapped it up in newspaper and put it into the cane basket from where Nenem had retrieved it and put it into the tin trunk before she was married to Kao.

Losi had very faint memories of her mother. She remembered her as being active and happy. She looked after the house and called out to the animals every evening in a particular tune that went something like 'Yu, yu! Youuue!' She swept the leaves and cleared the pineapple patch. She prodded the earth expertly and prepared it for planting ginger. That was what Losi remembered, though she also hinted that sometimes her mother appeared withdrawn, 'somewhere far away', but then she couldn't really be sure, she said, because she was a little child then.

In her heart, Nenem might have wondered sometimes at her own life, but she never spoke of the past before she met Kao. In the beginning there might have been a feeling of formality between husband and wife. Nenem, by nature, could be remote and unreachable, but Kao knew she was a passionate woman when she cried out and clutched at him. It was these moments that moved Kao. Sometimes their lovemaking was like molestation. He was tormented by thoughts of her past. He had seen her naked so many times and still she was shy. He watched her keenly, stripping her, exploring her, pulling her naked body up and she felt all his strength and passion entering her and expanding her womb. Yet when he spoke she closed her eyes to his pleading gaze and never told him what she wanted.

It was after the birth of Losi that Nenem became really close to Kao. Now she talked more, and sometimes she sang loudly in the house. This made Kao truly happy. He stared at his baby daughter and worried about her and Nenem so much that in the end he called for Nenem's mother to came and live with them for a while. The old woman was only too happy to oblige. She arrived, brisk and beaming, and spent every moment of her stay with her granddaughter. She fussed and suggested so many things that Kao began to be afraid until the old woman told him that nothing could happen to the child, for she was blessed, through her mother, by the great spirits. 'Hush!' she crooned, 'Hush! A treasure, a treasure! Whose little baby are you? Your mother came from the land of fish and stars! Oh little baby, go to sleep. Hush...'

Nenem, apparently, was a gift from the mythical land among the stars that was the dwelling place of a beautiful bride, also known as the celestial aunt, who came down to earth to bless the civilization of men with wisdom and grace. Nenem's mother had already lost two siblings before her and she had been worried that she would have no children. A shaman had been called and during an elaborate ritual he had invoked the spirits of the celestial aunt to bless the couple with a beautiful child. Some time later, the girl Nenem had been born.

Happy to be with her daughter and granddaughter now, the old woman showed no sign of wanting to return to her old man Sogong, who was shaky with drink but had enough strength and standing to call out to the village boys: 'Hey! Come and pick me up at once! I am here, at the bottom of the hill. Hurry up and bring a blanket with you!' She might have ignored him forever, so engrossed was she with the baby, had it not been for the earth silently sliding and shifting, preparing for an act of violence that was to change the lives and the landscape of the region for ever.

Late one evening all the villages of the land were startled by the thunder of hooves crashing through the jungle. Hundreds of mithuns had been running wildly to reach their owners and now they stood before the surprised villagers, snorting and trembling in a sweat of panic. 'What! Hai, look at the poor creatures...' the villagers were saying when the ground began to roll and tilt with a deep, angry rumble. The villagers peering out of their homes gasped to see the familiar outline of the hills tilting and swaying rapidly from side to side. The earth opened up and hills were swallowed as the savage quake shook the earth and tore apart huge chunks of forest.

It was one of the biggest earthquakes of the century. It measured 8.6 on the Richter scale and it came late on 15 August 1950. The river that Nenem had so loved was thrown off its course as a mountain collapsed and blocked its path. In a furious battle the river rose in a mass of churning, heaving water and swung inland, swallowing half of Pigo town. All the houses and the tree-lined avenues of the miglun quarter were gone forever. Then it swung west and spreading wider still it tore away every sign and symbol of the past years, and the school that Nenem had hated and the town itself were sunk beneath the floodwaters. According to the old people the tremors continued for many months and the town and the market place were covered with dead fish.

High in her new home Nenem heard the river roaring and might have imagined it was the sound of aeroplanes at war that David had described to her, or the waves of a sea. She became silent and Kao could see that she was shocked and saddened by this cruelty of nature. She clasped Losi and cried out every time the bed shook with the aftershock of the earthquake. Kao put a chain on the tin trunk and tied it to the thick wooden post so that it would not slip away. He stood by her and told her that a number of distant villages had been buried under massive landslides and that many people had lost their lives. In their vicinity the houses of so many villages had collapsed. But he assured her that because the buildings were so light, built only with bamboo and wooden posts, no one had died. The only injury was to old man Bukku, who had been hit on the head with a bamboo pole, but then everyone said he deserved it because he had been missing from his own house that night.

It was a fearful time, and it was a sad time. Losi's grandmother wept and shouted for her old man who, however, was safe and mobilizing men on the other bank of the now unrecognizable river, to receive relief material. When the first airplane arrived with food and medicines the villagers had to level a strip of land and place perforated steel sheets on the ground to cushion the weight of the aircraft. Small riverboats floated away and men and women were marooned for days on sandy islets that rose or disappeared with the swelling tide of water. The land was changing, and with these changes lives were changing. Kao saw the river spreading like the sea and watched the sun where it fell into the distant waters. Nenem stared at the restless, agitated land and her eyes scrutinized the broken line of the hills. Once upon a time a tender radiance had mapped these hills and the river...

It seemed her heart died very quietly.

One day, a few years after the earthquake, Nenem went as usual to the water point just beyond the orange trees. She felt dizzy and sat down on the wet stones sighing with wonder at the glittering leaves of the trees. It was the wind that carried her away, they said. She must have lain down and surrendered without a struggle because when the women found her she was already stiff and cold. The first thought that struck the two women was what to say to Kao. They rushed to another village elder's house and gasped out the news. Kao was away in the new grounds looking at some construction work for an office building that would make Motum the circle headquarters of the area.

'We must tell him immediately,' the old man had said. It was a simple thing. Men and women died and the news was told to one and all as soon as possible. It was a mark of respect. But no one had expected Nenem would die so silently without a trace of illness, and no one wanted to be the one to break the news to Kao. In the end two young men ran all the way towards the high fields to look for Kao.

He saw them running up the hill and came down. He had only to look at their frightened faces to know that something terrible had happened. He didn't say a word but ran past them towards the village.

It is said that when a loved one dies those who mourn should not soil the passage of the soul from one world into another with tears. Those who remember say that it was the village that mourned Nenem's death more than Kao, because, collectively, every man and woman mourned for Kao as well. He was the one who was left behind, and he was cloaked in a thick cloud of silence that made many people think that he would lose his mind. When the body was laid out the women covered their faces and wailed. They scolded Nenem for going away so suddenly. She was still so young! Oh! What a beautiful woman you were, they cried. Look at you now, oh! Did you not want to stay longer as the beloved daughter-in-law of the village? Hai! This is our life! We do not know when our time will come. Go in peace! Go in peace! No other beauty will match yours in this world or in the next. Do you remember how we crossed the river so many times? Now don't look back. Go in peace!

The village was crowded with relatives and visitors who had travelled from afar. They walked in and out of the house and Nenem's old friends Yasam and Neyang took over the household to feed everyone and accept the cloth and gifts for the dead. Kao stayed away in the interior of the house. Rakut's father said that when he came for the burial his heart had been wrenched by Kao's sadness.

'The man was pretending. He was looking up into a mirror on the wooden post and he would not turn around to meet me. I just stood there looking at him pretending to comb his hair while he prepared himself to face me. It was terrible... I also wanted to shout and weep but you know, there are moments lived on unspoken terms, and Kao did not allow me to weep. When he finally turned around he greeted me normally and we started the preparations for the burial. Hai! I have never seen a man hold himself like that, but I knew then that he was growing stronger because he had accepted that he would remain inconsolable for the rest of his life.'

When Hoxo and Rakut had barged into Kao's house that night Kao had been secretly happy to see their fresh, young faces. It was some years since Nenem's death. He told the boys that he was planning to send his young daughter to the school in the town close to their village, and quite unreasonably this piece of information had excited Hoxo who, for the rest of his stay in Motum, began to visit the quiet house frequently and became very attentive to Kao's silent nature and unspoken words, just as Kao had once been in the Sogong household. Thus the two families were linked up like this and one day there was a great stir in the schoolhouse of the town when Losi crossed the river with her bags and books to take her place as the new entrant in the school register.

At this time many families were leaving the old home villages and converging on the town in search of open land for permanent settlement. Kao was one of the few who kept his distance and he never left the village again, choosing to stay by the side of his beloved Nenem who was buried in the grove of orange trees. From this vantage point he looked out across the land and saw the hills rising row upon row and sinking into the sheet of water where the river fanned out like an ocean. The land was under siege. Myriad forces were nibbling away slowly but surely at its very foundations: Soldiers of the new rulers of the land, armed bands who wanted their own lands to rule, plainsmen and their co-conspirators from the hills who came to bring down the old trees and flatten the hills. The roots of trees, clumps of bamboo, the hidden life forms in the ancient body of the earth were being uprooted. Kao noted all this with his meticulous eye for detail but nothing worried him in his patient stillness and memory of the past. 'Nothing changes that much,' he thought. 'The hours pass, the days go, and still love lingers while the mist covers the land and the rain drowns the hills. Today, tomorrow, what does it matter? Time moves on and to survive in one piece all one needs is the ferocity of a lion or the heart of an angel.'

He saw the children changing and learning new things, and he smiled when he heard them speak in a new tongue while writing words in new scripts that no one in the village could read.

Across the river, young men and women walked to a school that was more than a mile away from their homes in Duyang. They crossed small streams and hurried through a forest of tall trees and dense undergrowth that could hide tigers and leopards. Many years passed like this. Then, one day, Hoxo's mother decided to go and call on her husband's old friend, Rakut's father. The old man was still sturdy and well enough to pick a quarrel with his son who was beginning to show all the signs of a rogue dedicated only to idleness and flirting with the young girls. Rakut, at that time, was also a terrible prankster and a trick of his had already become the stuff of legend. Once, he had a fit on the way to school. He suddenly collapsed and rolled about on the leaves shuddering and twitching as if invisible strings attached to the treetops were pulling him apart. Of course, he was pretending. He wanted to scare the girls. One of them ran off screaming. The news reached Rakut's father who responded immediately by sending out a number of relatives to the aid of his son. Rakut managed to keep up the twitching right into the house. In fact, the difficulty now was how to stop! His father, an immense man, watched his son keenly. He was a little perplexed, perhaps, but the women were afraid and making a lot of noise so he lost no time in calling for the shaman. Rakut's twitching grew more acute. The spell broke when the time came for the householders to catch the black pig that was the expected requirement for the shaman to restore Rakut to his senses. All the squealing and thudding of feet made Rakut titter. The old man got wind of something and Rakut recovered fast enough to leap out of the house clutching his shoes and shouting at the top of his voice, 'Enough! Enough! Hah! Hah! Hah! Oh! This is too much!'

He stayed away from the house for days and his father did not look for him.

'Let him play in the forest,' he said.

Hoxo himself had been writing love songs all through the summer nights of rain and wind, and now he had a thick sheaf of these notes and songs. They were never addressed to anyone by name but Rakut knew and he began to shout out to everyone that Hoxo was going mad with love for someone whose face could only be described as a flower and whose body and limbs flowed like liquid gold. So when Hoxo saw his mother dressing her hair and smoothing her ga-le before leaving the house, he sensed that his fate was being decided. She had raised him strictly, with love and attention, and though she had never held long conversations with him nor been demonstrative, the watchful distance, for Hoxo, had been filled with a sure tenderness. Now his mother smiled at him and Hoxo felt his heart swell with love and respect for this wonderful woman who had kept him safe and happy and given him everything all these years, since the death of the man who had rescued him from the burning hills. Rakut's father was good enough to call on the maternal uncles of the village and they all set out for Motum to meet Kao. It was a simple matter. There was no enmity between the families, and Kao was an educated man who did not question the antecedents of the declared son of Lutor.

So it was that one February day the young Hoxo stood on the ferry and saw the green wall of the opposite bank approaching him. It was the colour he remembered and loved, and when a gust of wind whipped the green bamboo into a delicate dance his happiness was complete. In those days the ferryboats carried chickens, goats, people, everything. A bridge or two had been built, and many more, bigger ones were built in later years, but the ferry remained the best method of crossing the river, as it is even today. The bridges spanning the river have all at some time or the other been torn away by flood waters and the land is dotted with old bridges standing derelict over sandy dunes where the river has changed course so many times.

When Hoxo and his party arrived Kao received him with great joy. His life too was tied up with the village of Duyang, after all. So many of his days had been spent sitting in the house of Sogong, waiting for Nenem to recover from her old wound and learn to love him. Now their daughter was being given away in return as a daughter-in-law to that same village. Losi was a very young woman but she carried herself with inherent grace. And as everything was settled with the blessings of all the elders and family clans, Hoxo carried away Losi, daughter of Nenem, across the river again. Apart from the wedding gifts of beads, brass vessels and metal plates that every bride takes with her, Losi also had in her possession the old tin trunk that contained the only tangible mementoes of a vanished past.

a matter of time

Remember, because nothing is ended
But it is changed

a matter of time

Remember, because nothing is gained
But it is changed

the old man and fires

◀◀◀◆▶▶▶

In the season of growing cabbages the ground is cold and hard. The tender leaves stoop under the wind and spring towards the light when the sun appears. The old man tended them with single-minded devotion. He looked up at the trees and wondered if they were closing out the light. He checked the hard bark for insects that might devour the growing leaves. He peered around for worms and bugs. In one corner the small patch of garden was fenced in with sugar cane. A wild bougainvillea crept over the wall of the house at the other end, and spurted glowing purple flowers every summer. Now it was a thick, bare coil that appeared dusty brown and dead. Everything was dry and bony, and ragged.

'I should clip them back,' the old man thought, looking at the young leaves, 'and prepare stakes to hold them up.' But his strength seemed to fail him these days.

Once, he had been as strong and tireless as the big river. How many times he had crossed that great expanse of water with his books and his art, and a zest for living. A fellow student had turned his life upside down. She had come to him like a bright dream that promised everything. He was from the mountains. She was born in the island of fishermen far to the south. A hundred rivers and streams separated their people but they had shared their loneliness in a season of discovery that had shut out everything and consumed them like an increasing fire. He was strong and determined, and she was equal to all his needs.

Then, one day, the unexpected happened. He was lying next to her in his small student's room when she said, 'I have to go away, you know.'

He didn't believe her. He thought she was just saying these things to tease him, or to alarm him, for these were the rituals of love. Yes, yes, he had thought, waiting for her next words.

'I am getting married.'

He realized that he was holding his breath. She stared back at him and then suddenly gulped and turned her face away. He knew she was weeping and he was terrified.

'Why? What is wrong?' he tried to touch her and she wept harder.

'I didn't tell you because I thought everything would be sorted out. I said I wanted to study! I told my brother but he has come all the way here to fetch me! The boy's family wants to see me immediately.'

'Refuse them!' he wanted to shout. 'I'll go and speak to your brother. You stay here. Don't move!' he wanted to say, but his voice was gone. He was crying and talking in his mind. He felt pain and fear rising and rolling in his blood like a silent tongue of fire.

The old man was a secret arsonist. If he saw a pile of leaves today the urge to set it alight rose in him like an urgent desire. The flames would leap up and he would be consumed with the taste and scent of acrid smoke and ash. Ah! It reminded him of so many things.

In his village littered with rocks, fires were lit all the time. He saw the ghostly flare of stars arcing from the brow of the hill and falling into the deep valley. 'They are the ghost spirits of husbands travelling to visit their brides,' it was said.

Now he saw his first love again, sitting up and looking at him. Her pale face was streaked with tears but her eyes were changed. She was looking at him and something was turning in his head. He was trying to remember, to find out something he had missed. What was missing in this relationship? What had she told him in their first meetings, in those early days of love? He could not recall any mention of another man. He thought she was too young, nobody would have expected her to be pledged to someone already! A thought crossed his mind. Maybe it was the sister! He remembered her telling him of a sister who was a bit strange. She was not violent, she was not deformed, but their community knew she was ill because on some full moon nights she would run out of the house completely naked. When they coaxed her back to the house she would be covered in sweat and it was an embarrassment to the family to see her beautiful body, and they would rush to cover her nakedness against the lascivious gossip that circulated everywhere. Maybe, he thought, his love was afraid that if she did not accept this offer people would link her with her sister and no one would want to marry her, thinking the madness might rub off on her.

'I'll marry you!' he wanted to say. 'Now! Let us go and sign whatever has to be signed.' But deep in his heart he knew it was impossible. A flame hissed. A picture of his mother standing on the long veranda flashed before his eyes. He had no money. He was living on a government stipend and if he married now he would be totally cut off from his village, his books, his inestimable academic life. He had crossed rivers and plains to reach this city that offered the only established academic institution in the whole region. He had sacrificed everything and willed himself to study just so that he could beat the old home in the village and exorcise the memory of hardship and poverty that he and his mother had faced all these years. He thought he would die. He cursed society, and he cursed his destiny. So poor! So poor! With nothing to eat and nothing to wear. On so many days he and his friend had walked to school barefoot, and sometimes used slippers made of wood and bicycle tyres.

The girl was still watching him and her eyes had changed again, till he felt he could not recognize her anymore. A searing heat coiled itself around his heart.

At the time his friend Abo had said, 'Let it go. Let go. Things happen. We know what fate is: the gods overrule us.'

So one part of his life ended. He never saw her again after that day when she climbed into a hand-drawn rickshaw with her small shoulder bag. He had seen her place her feet on the tin trunk that contained everything she had, and everything that they had shared. Even at the last she had looked at him as if trying to penetrate a great mystery. Then she had smiled and waved proudly as she left him for ever. He convinced himself that her proud smile was her way of saying that yes, they had loved each other. That was sufficient for him. They had loved one another. It was a way of coping with his pain. But deep in his heart he knew it was ash, and at best, the last embers of a jewelled fire.

He had married Nyameng, a simple village woman, and she had borne him sons and daughters and had been a great consolation to his poor, dead mother. He remembered how the old woman had always said, 'A good woman is a blessing. A good woman is a treasure beyond any calculation.' His mother had come to visit him once in the town where he was working. To humour her he had taken her to the big concrete market and there she had glared at the shopkeepers and bargained sharply for every purchase. She had bought an unusual piece of bright cloth with tasselled ends. She had had it wrapped. Then she had said, 'This is for Nyameng. We have been very lucky.'

Yes, he too had been lucky. He had travelled all across the land as an officer and had been well loved and respected for his upright dealings in the service. Throughout, his wife had provided rest and support. It was not a passionate relationship but it was comfortable and they made few demands of each other. Her quiet presence soothed him with the warmth of a simple household fire. Now if his bones ached a bit in the winter she rubbed him with hornbill fat and said, 'There! That should keep you fit.'

He smiled to himself. How quickly everything passes, he thought, listening to his wife's voice calling out to him.

'I'm here,' he called back, leaning his stick against the tree and moving towards the house. The widow of his old friend Abo had come on one of her visits.

It was a year ago that he had heard about Abo having taken to his bed with some complaint. 'Why, what's wrong with him now?' he had thought. Abo had always been tough as nails; just the other day he had been cutting wood and talking about going fishing. 'Must be old age,' he had told himself. Then one morning they told him his old friend was dead. 'Ah,' was all he said. The news did not surprise him. He knew the end was coming when Abo had started laughing in his sickbed remembering the days when they had walked to school together. That was well over half a century ago! He himself was almost stone deaf now but he could hear those memories weaving in and out of his head as clearly as if they had happened yesterday.

Now he looked closely at the old widow and remembered her anger and anguish during the period of Abo's illness. 'There is no need for him to be taken to the town,' she had said. 'It will be of no use.' The hard words had surprised and hurt him. But the wife had said, 'He's been talking like he's never talked to me before. Every morning he tells me a story of his past.'

And so it had been as she wanted. In the village they lit big fires for Abo, and in a small shack that marked the grave a fire would be kept burning all day and night for up to a year as a ritual of cleansing and farewell. He himself had been too old and weak to attend the funeral of his friend. But in his heart he knew the true reason: he was afraid. Everyone in the village had gone away one by one, and now he was the oldest of a generation that had opened up the land and had sat in the hot sun talking to unknown men and their tribes in small villages unmarked on any map.

There, he could see the line of porters slipping and straining up the steep slope with their packs of salt, rice and tobacco. He was back in time again, forty years, may be fifty, when he had left his home village and joined the new frontier service whose officers were opening up the land for administration. He saw one man carrying his tin trunk proudly emblazoned with his name in bold white letters and this filled him with a determination to reach the post buried in the wilderness of hills that stretched before him like endless waves. He had thought then, 'If men from the distant cities can come so far to live and serve in these remote outposts, why should we not do better, being natives of this land?'

They had trekked into the deepest mountains, lit big campfires in the middle of the forests to keep wild animals away during their night halt. One night he had awoken with an unimaginable fear clutching at his heart. The fire was almost burning out. The dogs were awake but they were crouched in absolute silence. It was eerie. Everyone felt the presence of something enormous, and the instinctive reaction of every man in the camp was to signal for silence in the face of this heavy, looming presence that was equally silent. It was a herd of elephants standing stock still against their shack of bamboo and caked mud. He shifted his eyes slowly and saw the slow swinging movement of a grey pendant trunk through the wide crack pressed against his face. The creatures were barely an inch away from where he lay. Any movement now, a cough or a sigh, might turn them on him. He didn't know for how long he lay like that. Just before the sun touched the treetops, they vanished. The camp men did not speak as they looked at the footprints and the droppings still steaming in the early light.

Now he could look back and say, 'Yes, we were brave. We obeyed orders carried to us by runners from one end of the world, and we marched into the other, wild corner. We did our duty.'

His memory moved back and forth like this, shifting, remembering and forgetting. In between he remembered the words of the young men when they told him about Abo's ill health.

'We have decided not to send him to the hospital in the big town. There is no point. We will watch over him here and perform the rituals. If he recovers, well and good, otherwise it is better he stays here and gives us his final blessings and words of advice.'

At the time he had thought that no effort should be spared to save a life, but now he felt relieved that his friend had not died in a strange place surrounded by strangers. When the end comes it is better not to be alone. It is not a time for individuals.

It is better for fathers and sons to follow in the footsteps of their ancestors.

'He was so talkative,' his friend's wife kept saying. Now that the crisis of illness and death was over the old widow was also eager to talk and talk. 'God knows, he spoke about the trees, and the placement of stones, and the ferry boats across the river.'

The ferry used to take them across to the town where the two friends attended school, and from where he later took an overnight bus and then a train to the city where he studied to become an officer. The ferry-boat owners were sharp businessmen already and the two friends winced each time they had to part with four annas to pay for the crossing. Once a storm had swept the boat downstream and they had almost lost their lives. Abo had flung away his bag of rice and bundles of dried fish. 'Hurry up! Hurry up!' he had shouted. 'Quick! Throw everything away!'

He saw the small basket of oranges he had carried from the village float away. Then they had clutched their books and jumped into the water to reach the first sand bar. A thick plank from here reached the bank and they landed there before the boatmen and crew herded the rest of the shouting, screaming passengers into smaller boats.

'If you have a mind you can live!' Abo had shouted, gleaming wet like an otter and shaking his books in the air. They were both so skinny at the time that they had a joke about themselves carrying salt in the hollow of their collarbones for the lemons they ate on their way to school. He was almost laughing out now. It was a glory to remember such things!

Perhaps old Abo was sitting on that rock now and squinting at him with a sly smile.

'Hey! What have you got to eat today?'

'Dried fish!'

'Hmm. Lets eat now!'

And on other days: 'Hey! What have you got to eat today?'

'Only rice.'

'Hmm. We can eat later!'

The afternoon turned to gold and the house was quiet and peaceful. When the sun sank behind the big hill a pale, translucent light flooded the western sky. It is the same wherever we go, the old man thought. Time impresses us when it is past. The clouds are always searching. The stars send their signals. Ah! If everything could be clear before the sun goes down.

The old woman had fallen into a heavy slumber and woke suddenly, wondering if it was morning. She eased out of bed with effort and was surprised to see her husband walking briskly past the window carrying a long bamboo pole. Slowly the aroma of burning leaves scented the evening. A big fire was crackling in the garden. A cloud of smoke billowed out across the shrubs and the sugar cane stalks and fanned out upwards as if to clear the air of bugs and insects. The bamboo pole was propped up against the tree and the old man was bending low and throwing in twigs and branches with the firelight aglow on his concentrated face.

the road

<<<<◦>>>>

From the houses furthest up the hill in Duyang, the town of Pigo, the oldest settlement in the region, is a few scattered rooftops seen through patches of dense vegetation. The first men and women who came here had started their journey from the mountains and walked through the forests carrying bamboo flares. They followed the green-and-silver vein of the river, convinced that it was the only road that would lead them to a destination. At a point opposite the spot that would later become Pigo, they stopped. They stared across the water and saw how the land was level and fertile. They cut plantain stems and lashed them together into rafts to get across. This was the origin of Pigo as a small landing stage on the right bank of the river.

It was a magical place. To the south the hills flattened and sank into the land of unknown strangers; but to the north and east the hills sloped gently and ranged themselves row upon row as if to shield the fertile valley from the wild mountains from where they had come. Orange trees grew here, the bamboo was young and rain-washed, and all the families who arrived moved in a daze of wonderment, exploring the streams and rocks, memorizing the green stillness and walking through the forest, following the same paths where the elephants wandered remembering their ancient routes.

Much later, Pigo became the first choice of the British officers in the area, and for a while it was the only town in the region with tarred roads and concrete buildings and electricity and daily bazaars.

The villages at the far edge of the Duyang cluster, however, from where the domain of the tallest hills and the most secret mountains began, had little connection with Pigo. They remained mysterious and remote even long after the British left. They were beyond time. Till the road came.

~

The village had never heard of anything like it before. Their granary doors had been broken and all their precious beads and jewels stolen. It had happened at night. The thunderstruck victims could not imagine how anyone could have done such a thing.

'It is like the work of spirits.'

'Maybe it was the spirits.'

'Who else would do such a thing?'

'Don't blame the spirits. Only men do such things!'

In these villages, the granaries were grouped together and built on stilts with a heavy circular piece of wood, like a wheel, attached to every post. This was to keep the rats out. All the grain for the year was stored here. The wealth of a family in the form of old beads, brass bracelets, marriage gifts and huge urns of beaten metal was also stashed away among the mounds of rice, millet and maize. Never in living memory had anyone tampered with these houses. The granary was sacred property and it was taboo to enter one without the consent of the owner. Doors were simply jammed shut with a bamboo stick, and only recently had a few families taken to locking them.

'If not the spirits, then who?'

'It could be anyone.'

The village seemed to stop breathing. The clear air shimmered and the longhouses shone like crouched monoliths with their fringe of wild plantain neatly trimmed over the narrow doorways. From her dark door Issam jangled a bunch of iron keys.

'Everything is gone,' she called out, 'but they didn't break the lock. They pulled out the planks! What is happening to our village!'

This was the last village on the administrative map. Anyone looking at the hills from the highest point in it would see the river coiled like a shimmering snake in the still, green jungle, beyond which rose a forbidding knot of mountains. It was a landscape out of a dream, and though an onlooker might pause and get his bearings, sooner or later the impenetrable vastness would trouble his thoughts. Across the river the white sand banks stretched and narrowed, before they were swallowed by the darkness where spiked bamboo stood in silent columns.

The village had moved to its own quiet rhythm for centuries, with old certainties and beliefs, but the road was changing all that. It had been over a year now, and the road was still being built. It ran up the mountain like a broken ladder of crumbling earth stained with iron ore. The red gash turned in great loops and bends and plunged into the heart of the far mountains, trying to reach the scattered villages buried deep in the land of mist and wild chestnut.

Very few locals took this ragged road. People had heard of

the mad woman who appeared by the stream made red by the gouged-out earth and threw bits of shale and rock at travellers. There were also whispers that the road was inauspicious. Everyone believed in the story of the red pool, the colour of blood, where ghostly fish swam round and round wearing bells that tinkled and drove strong men to acts of murderous violence. In the summer rains the road was crushed under falling rocks and boulders. The villagers clambered over them and laughed loudly, wading through the sticky red mud: 'What a place! At this rate we will never see progress!'

'I promise you a road by the end of the year!' Duan, son of Kedu, had said. He was a young man whose name had brought recognition to the village as the home of the youngest elected member to the state assembly. There was no doubt about his sincerity to serve his people. He had spoken with conviction and the villagers had listened, eager and happy in his victory, for it was true that till now their village had exerted its presence only in rather dubious ways, like the time when eight children had died of measles (brought, the villagers were convinced, by visitors from the town).

Another distinction of the place was the old school, acknowledged by one and all as the first school established in the region. But that was long ago, and since then the building had stood unchanged high up on the open plain above the village. And higher up there were fields of opium poppy aglow with flowers and milky sap. Apart from this, there was little to recommend the village.

So the villagers had heard Duan mesmerized by images of a road, vehicles and long rows of electric poles linked by taut black transmission wires. There would be progress. There would be new schools and their children would learn about the world in the new brightness that would pierce their dim homes like a sharp ray of light. Everyone had applauded and stepped forward to help.

Duan had led the way and now, every day, the hills echoed with the sound of heavy trucks bumping and screeching up the hillside carrying iron and cement. They scraped the riverbed for sand and blew up rocks that hung over the cut earth, threatening to smash the bulldozers and workmen who blew whistles and ran like ants on the edge of the mountain. New faces appeared among the foliage. They came from far away. Rows of bamboo shacks sprang up along the opened earth and smoke billowed out in dense plumes as the labour force settled in. A bamboo tube drew the perennial moisture trickling down the crevices into a source of water better than any tap in the towns. Big boulders strewn about served as laundry stones where naked children played in rain or sun, and women bathed and smiled at passing men who stared at the wet clothes that clung to their bodies.

A seductive new challenge emanated from these shacks. As the road stretched further with the oil and sweat of black fires and coal tar, the worker-women distilled the dregs of carbide and mountain rice into a witches' brew that turned the men of the village into feverish addicts roaming the nights with a yellow light glinting in their eyes.

Every night Issam lit the kerosene lamp and hung it on the wooden pole fixed securely over the door. She tried to sleep. But the night was unnaturally still. She wondered if someone was standing near the door waiting to break in. She strained to catch any unusual sounds and coughed loudly to deter imagined assailants. Sometimes a gecko cried and she jumped.

'It's agreeing with me! I should check the lock.' She stumbled out of bed.

'What is it?' her husband looked up irritably.

'I thought I heard a sound.'

'What sound?'

'Someone…something…did you hear someone coughing?'

'No.'

'But listen…'

'Then go and see. Take the torch.'

Haaah! At such times she wished she were a man. Then she would show him what it was to be a real man, instead of lazing under the covers not knowing whether there were robbers or an earthquake. Their houses were not safe anymore, everyone knew that. Why, she had heard that young boys were robbing the supermarkets in town and teenagers were extorting money and riding away on stolen motorcycles. In the plains, migrant workers prowled at night planning burglaries and murder. Now they were here. Houses were marked.

And she was the one, she alone, who had to be on the lookout to defend their homes, hearth and property!

So every night, unable to sleep well for the anxiety, she cleared her throat loudly and shuddered with resentment as her husband slept peacefully. The thin line of lamplight under the door comforted her. She turned her head so that she could watch it properly. If a shadow fell across that beam she would know someone was standing there, outside their door, waiting to hear if they were asleep. She glanced around quickly and was reassured to see the stout stick in the corner, ready for use.

'Better to be prepared,' she thought bitterly, as her eyelids began to droop.

After the theft in the granary buildings, it was evident to Issam that her fears were not unfounded. The road was bad news.

'I knew something would happen,' she said to the villagers gathered by the road. 'But of course no one listened. Now we have burglars among us! And who are we to blame?'

Everyone looked at each other. News had already reached Duan, and he was to come to the village by the afternoon to address the distressed people.

~

In her father's house Mayum pulled out her green velvet blouse and held it up. It was her one piece of fancy clothing that she kept folded under the mat so that it would not crease. 'I'll wear this,' she thought.

A brief meeting at the district town centre had convinced her that Duan had not forgotten what had passed between them before he was elected and work called him away to the capital. They had grown up together, seen each other walking to the fields almost every day and performed all the rites of the seasons like the other young men and women of the village. Even when Duan left to study in the town they were never far apart because he would come back to the village every weekend. He would move around with his friends then, and she with hers, and they would exchange words and looks that kept them laughing and happy all through the long summers before he contested the elections and became famous and the crowds pressed in on him and escorted him away.

And now he was coming back!

She had heard Issam's angry, mocking words and recognized the spite in them. She had felt a rush of anger towards Issam and others like her who were intent on harming and ridiculing Duan. She had said a prayer for him.

This morning, she had heard old Luda saying that they should press for an inquiry and catch the culprits. Everyone had cheered. But first someone must draft a letter to Duan,

Luda had added, so that their misfortune would be on record.
At this point all eyes had turned to Yomin, the schoolteacher.
He was the only one in the village who could read and write
more than a few sentences.

'What shall I write?'

'Write that all our jewels were stolen and that we want
action!'

'Whom shall I address it to?'

'To Duan, who else?'

'No, no! Send it to the minister.'

'No, it will get lost.'

'Just write it! Duan can carry it to the minister.'

'How do you know?' Issam had shouted quite loudly.
'How do you know he will? See, he promised us water and
nothing has been done. Where is the water? The labourers are
drinking it all up! I mean...Duan is our own boy, but after all,
he can't do everything!'

'Hai!' another voice had said, and then someone else had
disagreed, and for the first time in the village voices had been
raised in dissent. The elders and young men had begun to
argue.

'Where is the electricity?'

'He has promised us electricity, we'll get it.'

'Yes, but the contract has gone to others!'

'Hai! Who in the village is going to get anything of the
contract?'

'No one!'

'But we *will* get the electricity!'

'But why give the contract to others?'

'Why! Why!'

'What is this?' Suddenly the voice of Luda had silenced
everyone. 'We are *all* involved. Listen! What is wrong with

everyone? We have sown grain together and we have reaped harvests, and we have survived. Now stop sowing poison! Let us present our case. We will hear what Duan has to say.'

Then, to defuse the situation, he had pressed the young men on errands here and there, tapping with his stick all the time. 'Lucky I didn't leave this in the granary,' he thought, looking at it now. It was an old stick that had been a spearhead once, with a decorated shaft worn smooth with use. It was ancestral property. Every village elder possessed one and it was an indispensable prop in any kebang because it was believed to be imbued with special powers to aid the oratory of the speaker.

It was afternoon when a line of three vehicles arrived in a splatter of mud and came to a halt in the school ground just outside Mayum's home. The village children came running, leaping over the stones and yelling at the top of their voices. The car doors swung open and everyone stopped, waiting. Some boys they had never seen before jumped out and began to string up wires connected to a megaphone.

Mayum heard Duan's voice. She came out onto her veranda. 'My dear Mothers! Fathers! My brothers and sisters!' The voice crackled and hissed but it was his voice, raised a little now. She strained to catch every word and stayed very still.

'I have come because you called me. I have come because I am concerned. This is my home. I was born here. These stones, these mountains, this dust, this earth, it is in my blood. All of you, all of us, must work together to bring progress to our village, our beautiful village!'

Old Luda began to nod and clap, sticking his head up and looking around at everyone.

'A terrible thing has happened.' Duan said. 'Such a thing has never happened before, I know, but there is the law and we will see that justice is done. We will leave no stone unturned to solve this case.'

'All my jewels have gone!' someone cried out.

'It must be the labourers!' someone else called out.

'Who else?'

'The road builders.'

'I say the road is a bad thing!'

'Soon they will kill us!'

'Hai, hai! Don't utter such words.'

'But all my jewels are gone!'

From her veranda, Mayum looked across at Duan. She saw his face, serious and attentive. Everyone knew he was a good man, but as Luda had said so many times, honesty and goodness were of no use in the world Duan had entered. To get things done a person had to use stealth and patience, like setting a trap. 'You must know your prey. And who is your prey? Why, us! The people, of course! You have to lure us like fish, like deer. You have to use words sweet like oiled wood. Oh ho! ho!' Luda often said, 'The ways of the wily grow like a vine.' Mayum wanted to argue with him, but he was a village elder and she seethed quietly. On such days, she feared for Duan and wished she knew how to shield him from so much bitterness.

Now Duan was saying that the electric poles had already reached the village. The workmen would follow to set them up, and department engineers would be arriving to supervise the work. Then there would be telephone lines as well. But before that he would personally carry their letter to the minister in the capital and see that the thieves were caught and punished.

When the discussion ended and a line of young women dressed in their brightest clothes and necklaces of silver began the welcome dance, Mayum turned her back on the spectacle and went into the house. Behind her, the women clapped their hands and chanted:

Welcome, welcome
Within the circle of these hills, brothers!
Let us live together.
In the shelter of these hills, sisters!
Let us live together.

Far below the village a group of young men stood in the shade of the big trees. Any passer-by would have easily identified them as the sons of one family or another, but everyone who would recognize them was at the meeting. The young men were talking about the theft of the jewels and their faces were hard and set.

Larik, son of Togla, was the most animated. 'He has no idea about the situation,' he said, referring to Duan. 'He thinks if we wait and be patient the government will reward us. Reward us with what? This one terrible road is all they have managed for us in fifty years! And what does it bring us? Outsiders. Thieves. Disease. Will this road bring us good health? A new school? Look at the one we have now. The first school built in the region—but has anyone showed any interest? Wait, they say all the time. Everything takes time, they say. But I tell you, I have seen the roads in the capital and they are worse than the one they are building here. If they cannot tidy up there what guarantee do we have that they will give us anything good here, especially when they don't know or bother to find out who we are and how we live!'

Larik was speaking with such anger and urgency that his friends were spellbound. Everything he said was true. Every day they saw their village elders fading before their eyes. They were turning into shrivelled stick-men who sat at home all day sipping rice beer and wasting away. The old days of war and valour had vanished. They had surrendered ancestral lands to the government and now the road and the things that came with it seemed to be strangling them and threatening to steal their identity like a thief creeping into their villages and fields.

'We deserve better,' Larik was saying. 'We deserve more than words.'

The group stood talking for a long time, then climbed up and joined the meeting. They stood behind the line of children and women.

'Where have you been all this time?' Luda jumped at them.

'We were down by the river.'

'What! You are the ones who should be helping Duan. It's a lot of work, all this business of governments and ministers.'

'We are ready to assist,' Larik said tersely.

Mayum prodded the fire and pretended to be very busy. Duan had stepped into their house to call on her father.

'Give the young man a drink!' her father said.

She poured the rice beer. She carried the mug to Duan and saw his old smile as he accepted her preparation.

'There is so much work to be done,' she heard him telling her father. 'You must keep the youth together. Don't let them take the path of violence.'

'It is not in our tradition to be violent,' her father said.

'No, I know. But in the town they say our village is the most intractable of the lot. They say we don't want to help ourselves. That we only know how to protest, hah! hah! But wait, another few years and we will be a model village. Once there is transport and communication everything will open up and then we will see what potential we have. I have said I will take up this case and I will move heaven and earth to get to the bottom of it, but no one must take the law into their own hands.'

The old man laughed. 'You take care,' he said. 'You know,

your father was a great orator. Your clan root is "oratory", and
I will tell you this: words are important. You can change a
man's thoughts by the use of the right words. I know, I know,
where you live they think we only sit around the fire and talk,
but this is our business. Words can solve riddles and transform
a life. Our village is very old and patient, don't worry.'

Duan nodded. Then they were both silent as they stood
together drinking their beer. The house creaked with the weight
of people and Duan said, 'I have to go, otherwise we will miss
the ferry.'

He looked at Mayum. 'I will return with the jewels!' he
said, his eyes bright with hope and laughter.

The village was fighting a grim battle. A stubborn pride wrapped
around the young men like a dark cloak that kept them
screened from the rest of the world. They did not welcome
strangers. They did not want to join hands with the government.
We are not seekers of fortune, they said. We are not seekers of
words. We are not seekers of a new identity. Leave us alone.

One day, with the big clouds spread over the village, the
young men travelled swiftly, slipping over the mud, traversing
the hills through the old trail that was the original path before
the road was roughly aligned to follow it. They crossed the high
fields of opium poppy and cut across the debris of shale and
rock, following the red stream. They forked out by the red pool
and scrambled up the steepest path of fern and haunted trees.
Now they could see the dark silhouette of the labourers'
bamboo shacks and the bulk of the bulldozer pinioned against
the mountain wall. It was threatening to rain like a storm, and
they redoubled their efforts.

Larik had planned carefully, like a master strategist who
had fought many battles before and led his men to victory. This

time, too, they would not lose. A tin can with a small plastic hose doused the road with the fumes of burning. A blue flame hissed and spread rapidly in a rippling line of waves racing towards the drums of coal tar and the sleeping shacks. Larik signalled, and the busy shadows vanished before the first cries of alarm went up.

High above the road a monstrous overhang of rock began to move and crack. A fissure appeared in the earth that thrust up the roots of the old tree as it heaved and swayed. The tree made an indescribable sound as it fell, and Larik thought, 'The old tree is weeping.' It hurtled down the mountain but before it hit the road Larik and his group had disappeared into the night.

The restless village was the focus of attention again.

'The culprits! Who has done such a thing?'

Luda and his circle tried to restore order. They looked carefully for an exchanged look, a secret smile, a careless word. They could gather nothing. The only answer they could give when the wireless message finally arrived asking them for a report on the situation was that they would call a kebang again, before anything else.

'What, another meeting! How many meetings are we going to have?'

'Don't worry, it's just acting,' Issam said dryly.

Not so long ago the kebang was the shining institution of these villages that solved all disputes and dispensed justice. Under the shade of the trees a group of men would assemble carrying their well-worn sticks and they would all be men recognized for their knowledge and honesty, their courage and their powers of oratory. Sometimes a case could drag on for years and even carry over into the next generation. Yet there was always a council of men to take over and assemble again under the trees to distil words, explore human psychology, and weigh and measure right against wrong in a long exercise of logic and compassion.

But things had changed now, and though Kebangs still functioned in many villages as traditional judiciary systems, they were losing their powers and giving way to the modern legal system, and all its failings.

Mayum thought of how the news must have reached Duan and what he must be thinking. He must be feeling let down, she thought. Despite the setbacks and false promises of so many years, despite his longing to live well and to achieve something, she knew that there was in him the will to do good. He would be hurt.

Words. Yes, there were words for prayer and invocation, for blessings, and words for negotiation and healing, but what words would there be now to say to him?

She wondered about Larik. She had seen him at the water point splashing water on his face and head. They too had known each other all their lives, but this time he had not acknowledged her. Instead, he had continued to wash and splash. Then he had looked at her silently and walked away, swinging his hands vigorously to shake off the water.

'What is happening now?' she thought.

Issam and Mumdi and all her friends were talking about the landslide that had smashed a chunk of the road and piled trees and shrubs over the burnt-out shacks. Another mystery was the theft of the electric poles. One pole had been fished out of the river, but all the rest were missing. If they were hidden in the forest it would take years to find them! Why had anyone done these things? Where would all this lead?

By the middle of the afternoon the storm crashed down on

the village. A sound like the sea at night fell with such force that it rattled the stones and shook the fringed thatch of the longhouses. Everyone ran for cover. Yomin, the schoolteacher, bolted the doors with their rickety locks and ran for his house. No school. No lights. No students! His bag of books flapped against his legs as he ran. The heavy drops of rain landed on his head and ran down his face as he jumped on a boulder and almost lost his balance. What a place!

Then he stopped and laughed loudly when he saw Luda prancing around stiff-legged before him, waving his stick and dancing in the rain.

What a place indeed. Hadn't it survived for so long? Wouldn't it survive these winds of change as well? Yomin was sure, or perhaps he wasn't. But everything seemed possible today in this little village as big as the world.

~

The news of the arson and theft spread like wildfire. It was carried on the wind, over the tops of tress and through the circling mist, alighting on the remotest of villages, disturbing the hearts of men and women. They had never heard anything like this before.

In the longhouse Larik and his friends sat around the fire and watched the flames. Nothing was finished yet; they would make sure it wasn't. The lights flickered and the old petro-max hissed and spat as old Luda gurgled on his pipe drawing in the opium fumes and ate big chunks of mashed rice in between.

'I had a dream,' he declared.

Everyone turned to him. The old man was a bit of a shaman and an interpreter of dreams.

'I dreamt,' he said, 'I was walking in an unknown land. It

was full of rocks. Ahem! Not a single tree nor grass or leaves. It was very frightening. Only rocks and rocks. Then I saw big red flowers blooming on the rocks!'

'Hai, you rogue. You are teasing us!'

'No, no. I saw flowers growing on barren rock.'

'Okay. So that was your dream?'

'Yes. And it means we will grow old drinking drinks and die in a state of happiness. Hah, ha ha!'

Now the girls who had been preparing themselves in one corner began to emerge, tinkling with jewellery. They too seemed to be in a mood for teasing and began to sing:

Oh, what is the matter
With our brothers?
Why are they not wedded yet?
Oh, can anyone tell us
Why all the young beauties
Run away from them?
Is it because they have
Thorns on their hands?

The sound of singing and clapping began to fill the house. Everyone was nodding, staring at the girls and the fire. Larik was thinking, Yes, the bridge is breaking, but nothing is over yet. He knew all the dying villages still waited for a singular paradox to resolve itself: All the first officers and public leaders who had worked so hard to distinguish their home villages had somehow turned their backs on these very villages. They had retreated into work in distant places and when a relative approached them for a favour they avoided the case because it would seem like nepotism, and to have their integrity questioned was a thing most damning to this clan. So while the small circle of achievers struggled with correct administration and were praised for their honesty, the home village itself was studiously ignored and granted no favours.

'The bridge is broken,' the boys would say metaphorically. In Larik's mind the bridge was the long crossing that had made these men noted government servants and officers. Across this divide the officers surrounded themselves with papers and a new script and hardly looked up from their desks. If they did, sometimes, they might notice a slight stirring on the other side. There, the dead were being buried, but these men had no time to take leave and be present at the village in proper custom. The youth were caught agitating, and there was no time to sit with them through the days and nights and ease their frustration. Yes, the bridge was swaying and slowly tearing away. Land was being stolen. Forests were being cut and logs floated away down the river. New fences marked old territory and it seemed a curtain had fallen over the old villages. What was once sacred, the old sense of joy, was being lost.

Yet Larik knew they would never give up on their elders. Their ancestors had followed the river and staked their claim on both her left and right banks. Never mind, now, that a whole generation was fading. If only they remembered, someday they would bridge this gap. If there was laughter and singing, like this, like this, he thought, yes! Then one day, inevitably, a new bridge would be built again and there would be a new crossing.

a portrait of sirsiri of gurdum

◄◄◄◄◉►►►►

Far away and much further downriver, closer to the plains of Assam, the old establishment of Kerang had swept up from the check post in the foothills and climbed haphazardly across the hills to the settlement of Gurdum.

Gurdum was new, and oddly perpendicular in shape. It crept halfway up the mountain and spread out in all directions. Small plots were divided into sectors, and new buildings clung to the roadside and protruded over empty space hanging over clefts and ravines.

The town was permanently awash in debris. Plastic floated across the hills, clung to riverbanks, perched on trees. Broken glass and discarded packaging scarred the bald slopes closest to the town. Workmen sucked on wet bidis and chipped away at the mountainside. Their women stood by and looked askance with dark, savage eyes. A row of labour sheds hung on to the hillside and here they lived, loved, bathed naked on the roadside, fought bitterly, and sometimes murdered each other. With their labour the new settlements were straining to expand against the rocky earth and rearing upwards, challenging the broken land and the falling mountains. The last row of lights reached midway up the mountains. Beyond this it was black as night.

Sirsiri lived in the top row of houses in Gurdum, and her sweeping glance passed like a compass over all that lay below her.

There was the single steep, slithering road that linked all the sectors and markets of the place. There was the bank and post office intersection. A few identical grocery stores were scattered here and there, and the road itself was worth only a few kilometres and was bereft of traffic signals or street lamps.

One could pass the whole day staring out of the window. By five o'clock, sometimes, the clouds would lift and the steep fall of the mountain would be visible. At such times the small town would appear to sway and lift with the force of the wind that would begin to build up from the northern side. This was also the hour that Sirsiri would feel the pull of an addiction that seemed to have hit everyone in Gurdum. If the phone rang at this time it meant someone was calling to say, 'Come over. Are you ready?'

Playing cards had become the grandest pastime and Sirsiri was the keenest gambler among a group of women who played as hard as the men. Some card groups played for days and nights, deserting their homes, offices and shops, even their small children. They were elated by their victories, bruised by serious losses, and they moved from house to house, the incorrigible regulars boasting about how much they had lost rather than about how much they had won. Serious drinking was expected on these occasions. Cars came and went. Some players fell asleep, then roused themselves to play again, refreshed by more drink and cigarettes. At these times it seemed the human brain functioned at an extraordinary plane. Men bragged that their minds were clear and razor sharp, despite the claustrophobic air and dim lights, the heavy haze of cigarette smoke and the lack of food, sleep and any sense of time. It was an addiction that heightened speech, laughter, and feelings of friendship. It veered minds towards nostalgia, philosophy and, more often than not, spiteful gossip and shocking disclosures.

'Do you know,' said Sirsiri, 'I saw Kalum the other day, driving that new woman teacher.'

'Really?'

'Yes. I think there's something going on.'

'What!'

'The way he was driving, saying something to her and the way she was smiling...I thought the car might run off the road!'

'Hai, come on! He must have been just giving her a lift.'

'Hah! I can tell about these things. I have a feeling.' And Sirsiri declared her hand of winning cards with a flourish.

Sirsiri had a narrow, swarthy face and restless, glinting eyes. She moved like a fly alighting swiftly and then darting off. She always left a place with a high, shrill laugh. When she wanted to be friendly she moved close to a person and shaped her lips into a half smile that was meant to suggest eagerness and concern. 'We never see you, where have you been hiding?' she would say. Or, 'Hai, you have been travelling? How lucky! I am the only one rotting here!' Then she would laugh and dart a meaningful look at her husband Pesso, a quiet man originally from Duyang, who smiled stoically at all her jibes.

Some fifteen-twenty years ago Sirsiri had come to Duyang as a young bride from a distant village. People said she had sung songs on the radio and that it was at the new, tiny Radio Station in Pigo that the young Pesso riding in on a bicycle to deliver mail had first set eyes on her. Soon old man Pator was spreading the happy news that a great singer was going to become a daughter-in-law of the village, and Sirsiri had been welcomed with great honour. Her husband Pesso was a good man. He owned plenty of land near the river and he was also employed in the government office. This raised his status in the eyes of all the people of Duyang. However, this had not impressed Sirsiri. She had other dreams, and no matter where she was, she always wanted to be elsewhere. She was unhappy even after Pesso sold his land in the village and moved to Gurdum for good. After the birth of two daughters and a son the shy young girl turned into a brisk, talkative woman and as the years rolled on and the children grew up, the Pesso household began to show signs of greater and greater strain.

Pesso never understood why she was always in such a temper. In their house, voices rose and fell at odd angles. They flew across the rooms, bounced off the walls and crashed from the ceiling. There were shrill voices and chanting voices uncoiling in a litany of complaints. Sometimes, lost strains of hidden music broke through, but this was rare. Usually, voices whispered urgently, pattered, shrieked and raged and swiped at objects and beings. Then silence rose like a dense wave that twisted meaning and context.

Talk. Talk. Talk. Sirsiri talked everything to death. Words rolled out of her mouth like a long tongue of vengeance. Her talk antagonized well-wishers and drove away visitors. In the end, it even drove Pesso out of the house. 'What did I say?' the poor man had muttered as he slipped out one day and stayed away for two days. Soon, this became a pattern and sometimes he would be gone for several weeks. He hardly realized that the root of the endless words lashing at the world was his very silence, and his lack of words to say to the woman he had married.

Sirsiri's complaints were loudest in the long season of rain. She cursed the sky and the mountains and her frustration grew as the rain poured down in sheets day after day.

When the rains stopped, the day sweated vapour and lethargy. Men ceased to think and sometimes, in a fit of madness, they rushed into the forest to hack away at the undergrowth and hunt with brutal instinct, killing three deer in one night. Others escaped to the big river, throwing their nets into the summer flood while their women waited, worn out at home. The men trampled the forest and shouted at the wind. They cut into the earth, removed the trees, ravaged the soft soil and wept in their dreams, not knowing for what or whom they mourned. The earth trembled under the burden of heat and rain. All the talk was about earthquakes.

'If one ever came, the place would go,' they said.

At night Sirsiri left her clothes just so, draped over a chair to be able to grab them and run out in an emergency. She dreamt of mudslides, and started at the sound of the late-night lorries. She made sure the candle was within reach, and aware that nothing bothered her husband, she worried about their investment in the shape of a concrete building now being raised in a steep place above the road. What if the road broke? What if the pillars collapsed? Everyone knew that workmen used sub-standard material all the time! She imagined the mountains folding and saw the tangled roots of trees upturned to the sky. She saw rivers of mud and the rising dust of fallen buildings and heard herself wailing in fear and frustration.

Oh! What a place! Cursed, ill-chosen, disturbed! A little clearing in the forest full of stones and rain! When everywhere else, cities were rising overnight like columns of light into the sky! Sirsiri was bitter and bored and nothing consoled her.

the golden chance

****◆****

One day I was sitting in the small bank building of Gurdum, staring out at the sloping road and thinking, 'Ah, now I must really start doing something worthwhile, I must work and save money and give something to my relatives,' when Kasup came in and sat down beside me. He greeted me loudly, then shuffled papers and began to talk earnestly with the bank manager. When I prepared to leave, clutching my account book with its puny, secretive numbers, he suddenly pushed back his chair too and said, 'Come, come, I want to ask you something.' He drew me to one side and bending close to me he said, 'Are you happy?'

What! I started. It was the last thing I had expected to be asked.

The days in Gurdum were clear and mostly calm. At night the wind moaned down the gorge and rattled the rooftops, and my sleep was full of vague dreams that unfurled like a mist. My papers and books lay scattered about and I liked the seclusion that allowed me to be indolent.

'Why?' I said to Kasup, almost whispering, as if I were guilty of something.

His wide, fresh face broke into a smile and I understood that because Kasup had travelled to the city recently his head had been completely turned by the sights, sounds and smells of the other life. The representatives sent to the National Development Council for Backward Areas had been thoroughly overwhelmed by the sea of people, the lights and the roar of traffic and they had returned triumphant, as if they had learnt the secret of modern life.

I nodded and made my way back to the little building I called my home. All summer my plans had been erratic. I was still landscaping, trying to fit the outline of the hills within the frame of bamboo and young foliage that surrounded my house. When the phone rang I jumped at it, just wanting to hear another voice. It was my friend Mona from the city and she was shouting at the top of her voice. 'I have been trying to reach you for days! Listen, someone wants to make a film. Can you help?'

'A film? About what?'

'About Duyang and the other villages! The place and the people. This is a golden chance! He's a very famous documentary film-maker. You better come down!'

According to Mona the film crew were working out the logistics and had already applied for their Inner Line Permits and other entry formalities. We just had to fit the pieces together—the storyline, the places to be filmed, and instructions to the would-be players about what to do.

'Why don't *you* prepare the itinerary?' she said with great enthusiasm. 'Tell them about the caves. About the bead mountain. But first speak to the villagers. I'm sure they will be interested. After all, it will be a golden chance for them too!'

I imagined people like Hoxo rolling their eyes. Appear in front of a movie camera? Sit on a rock, chant something? No!

Never! It would be too funny! Who wants to see us? Others, like Rakut, would be sure to say, 'Forget it! It will take a hundred years to get it right.'

I couldn't see what this golden chance was about, and why it had so gripped my friend. Huh! I had heard about chance and opportunities a thousand times, and actually there was nothing like that at all. Help some film crew? I wasn't sure. I sat on the cane sofa and put up my legs to think, staring at the TV screen. There was a Hindi film on, a fight scene out on the road, in the middle of honking, screeching angry traffic somewhere in Bombay or Delhi or some other big city.

The phone rang again. 'What are you doing! What are you doing?' I had almost forgotten! It was Omi and Dabo reminding me about the dinner at their place to celebrate Dabo's new play. It had not been staged yet, but we all knew the lines by heart, because whenever anyone of us felt like getting together, we met on the excuse of finalizing the play. Now I rushed out to buy something for the party. In the market they were selling fish buried in ice. These came packed in crates from distant states and the sellers lifted the gills swiftly for inspection, to check for freshness and superior taste. But there were only ten fish in a pile, the last of the heap, so I turned to the local products, which were livelier: Green leaves with thorny stems, slabs of preserved, moist bamboo shoot, camomile, bitter clerodendrum, wild berries of the belladonna family. The women were sitting in a row on open ground just as they have always done, with their baskets of greens, among the fish scales, the mud and ooze, and the men weighing live chickens.

Omi greeted me happily. 'Come, come in. Bless you!' Dabo also started up. There were many friends here already, and a delicious smell wafted in from the backyard. A group of young men and women from their village were handling the cooking, Omi said, and we were not to lift a finger.

'God bless them,' said Dabo of these clan brothers and sisters who travelled down from the hills like a migratory labour force in search of any old job to help them cope in these times of change.

Dabo has a full and untidy head of hair and works in a small cubbyhole of an office in the Weights and Measures department in the busy centre of Gurdum. Here, among the dusty files and the shrubs creeping up the stained and dusty windows, he imagines the sun and the moon thundering across the sky and writes and rewrites his unending plays where entire villages and the people of Gurdum town are the cast of characters.

His latest play, the one we were celebrating, was called *Sepek, Sepek*. The word implies the sound of a beating stick. Briefly, the play was about guarding food. Anyone would recognize the pointed face of the old lady who could be seen peering in through a door in the first frame...

She is the quickest woman in the village to raise her bamboo tongs in defence of her food, and there she is, bending over an inert, sleeping form. A rooster crows, to tell the audience that it is dawn. The thief gets no time to wake up and run before the bamboo tongs fall on him, repeatedly: Sepek-sepek-sepek! Next frame: The maid is now captured looking over her shoulder with hands stretched out, in a posture of lifting or taking something, and finally frozen in the act of drinking all the milk. She gets it, too: Sepek-sepek! The famous door bursts open again and another unfortunate is seen flying out. Sepek! Final cut: There she is again, the old woman, with a look of cunning triumph on her face. She is trotting towards the storehouse holding an enormous lock. Then she is heaving and locking up the place with a good turn of the key as large as a gun.

We laughed over this play and spent many hours outlining the old lady's set face with her eagle eyes and a short, round haircut.

'When is it going to be a hit?' Omi said. 'When are we going to rake in the m-o-o-lah!'

We were always imagining pots of money and lots of goodies. Dabo smiled sheepishly and said, 'Well, wait a bit. I want to set the characters right.' He told me that he had asked Sirsiri to act in the play and that he was trying to fit in a scene where Sirsiri could sing. 'Perhaps it will lift the play,' he said.

We knew what that meant. Sirsiri would make outrageous demands and the play would languish. Like many others Omi, too, found her intolerable. 'She's like a shrimp jingling with her beads and necklaces,' she said. On the other hand, we knew that Sirsiri's presence could add splendour to the play, because whatever one might say about Sirsiri, there was no denying that she had stage presence. And she could certainly sing.

'Well, whatever it is, just finish writing the play!' Omi now said.

Outside, the young helpers had taken over the kitchen and there was a big fire going in the backyard. The place was littered with bamboo shavings, leaves, baskets and roasting tomatoes and chillies. An iron grill covered with skewered pieces of meat was sizzling and dripping fat into the fire. A young boy of about eleven years was crouched near by, poking at the coals with a long stick. Now and then he held up the flaming end of the stick and stared at it. Then he pushed it back into the fire.

'Aiee! You'll burn yourself. Don't touch the fire so much,' shouted Omi.

'Really! This boy is too much. He's always playing with the fire!' A young man darted forward and gave the boy's hand a smart slap. Then he was grinning again, and went back to chopping and cutting and stirring and doing everything all at once. Omi told me he was Rigbi. They belonged to the same clan and he was the father of the boy. The boy also grinned and continued to throw in bits of paper and twigs into the roaring fire. They reminded me of another of Dabo's plays about a boy and his father from the village, a play that might well have been modelled on Rigbi...

The young boy. Today, perhaps, is the happiest day of his life.

His heart is humming with happiness. He is with his father and his father is cooking a lot of food. He sees the green onions, leaves, wild fern; and he wants to jump up, run, dance and sing. He takes a deep breath. The aroma of roasting meat! It is all he desires. Meat, bone, gristle, fat, skin! He remembers the taste of sizzling fat burnt black and dripping onto the hard rice, with bits of charcoal still sticking to it. He will eat it all. It is a taste he can never forget. The crackling would stick to his fingers as his mother watched. He cannot remember ever seeing her eating, and she never smiled, but in those moments he had seen some happiness glowing in her eyes, before she closed them forever one cold winter when the meagre crop in their fields had perished. Ever since then he has stayed close to his father who is still young and strong and dashing.

'We may not have much but we have this. Look!' His father would tap his head as if it contained great treasures. Sometimes he would roll up his shirtsleeve or flex a calf muscle and say, 'Look! We have this!'

His father chopped wood, played football, and sometimes the boy saw him struggling with papers and stamps as he pursued jobs and sent off one application after another. Now they are in the town, and nothing has changed. But his father says, 'No fear. We are close to the ground. If we climb very high and fall off we would break our backs! Hah, ha!'

The skinny boy laughs happily. One front tooth has broken off and he looks like a thin bunny rabbit. This endeared him to the old women of the village who scolded him for eating too many sweets.

'Hah, what sweets!' he would think in his tough little heart. For him, it was always about meat. His friend's father's drying rack was always full of meat. His friend brought strips of meat in his pocket and they would eat it while running over the stones. It hardened their jaws, the juices filled their mouths and flowed into their blood like the taste of wind, sunlight and salt. He could feel the light streaming into his eyes, stretching his limbs and changing his skin, teeth and bones until he thought he was turning into a tiger...

Now father and son were positioned near a big pot that was steaming and bubbling. It was a special pork curry that Rigbi was cooking with freshly ground turmeric.

'Rigbi loves to cook,' Omi was saying. 'God knows how he enjoys it, but he is always trying some new combination. Tribal modified, he says. I remember his old man was a big eater. He would throw a fit if he found the rice bins half full. Rigbi's wife, poor thing, had a hard time keeping the old man happy. I think the last years were really bad. She used to say her legs were cooked standing under the hot sun, knee-deep in water for hours on end, planting rice. Ai! It's backbreaking work!'

It was the hills breaking our backs, I thought. The steep slopes offered little. In the towns, rice, lentils, oils, everything could be purchased, but in the far flung villages every stalk of grain, every root of tapioca and every extra luxury like beans and cabbages was raised with backbreaking toil.

176 / the legends of pensam

'Well, earning money is no joke either,' said Dabo. It was no secret that he found no joy in his work, but his silent arena was filled with movement and thoughts of escape. And at least he had a roof over his head. In the villages it was quite different. Families clawed their way up black fields and lived with blackened hands and broken nails. Rigbi had fled from the village after the death of his wife and now they said he could marry again. He had a way with young women. No one protested, because everyone knew that all our days are like a small breeze that stirs briefly in the teeming green when the evening is filled with the cry of insects rising with desire before they die.

Dabo was saying, 'On the way to Rigbi's village you pass the land of caves. There are big caves and rocks dotting the place and they're full of bats. People say on our way south the tribes sheltered in these caves. The children grew up eating bats. *Tapon, tapon*, they cried. We want to eat bats!'

Ah! The caves again. And with this, the echoing voice of my friend talking of 'the golden chance'! I had heard about these caves in the hills far up to the north. The few people who had seen the place said it was a network of tunnels that opened into caverns wide enough to park five lorries side by side. They said when you turned off the torch the darkness inside was absolute, it was unlike anything in human experience. Perhaps the beginning of the world was something like that. Keyum. That is what we call that darkness beyond the reach of memory. And of course it was not god who created light; it was the spark of imagination that gave birth to light. This was the path of seeing. Now I pondered this. Maybe the film-makers would be interested in the caves, and in our stories of creation.

It was important to record our stories. The old rhapsodists were a dying breed, and when they were gone, who would remember?

What happens to the people and the places we forget? Where do they go?

Hah, who knows about these things, I thought.

Just then it was announced, 'Food is ready!'

A small feast was laid out before us. Chicken cooked in bamboo, turned on a slow fire. The delicate flavours of the petals of the plantain flower and Rigbi's secret herbs. Aromatic bamboo rice, each grain glistening in its paper-thin skin. Crushed berries liberally mixed with dried chillies and ginger paste. Everything was perfect. The cold weather had whetted our appetite. A sense of well-being and happiness spread like a warm glow in our bones. Perhaps the ancients were right after all. Delicious food, like beautiful form and melodious sound, is certainly one of the five attributes of the realm of desire.

Dabo, who was rummaging in the cupboard, whipped out a bottle containing a pale golden liquid. It was the distilled spirit of rice wine. 'Today is the day!' he said. It was heady stuff. The first sip was like a taste of nostalgia. Suddenly our youth glided past like a bright train at night, bearing the shining pieces of our lives like faces in the lighted windows. It is always like this; it is an intricate magic: we imagine the way to avoid regret is to do nothing, or try everything.

'Here it comes!' Now Rigbi came in holding the big pot of steaming, fabulous pork in front of him. He bent forward a little, and his boy ran up immediately and handed him a piece of cloth. Rigbi wedged it into the handle, and as we all looked eagerly, one end of the heavy pot lifted, and the other handle seemed to pull away and in an unbelievable, heart-stopping moment, slipped from his desperate grip. Then everything was flying through the air.

'W-A-AHH!' The pot clanged noisily, then shuddered into stillness. We had stopped breathing. No one moved. No one said anything. Dabo was holding his head and his eyes were shut tight.

It was the boy who was the quickest of us all. In a flash he had found an empty basin and was rapidly picking up the scattered chunks of meat and throwing them into it. He was concentrating fiercely, brows in a tight knit, and he was breathing hard, as if he was choking.

Omi rose, as if from a dream. 'I don't believe it!' she cried. 'How could you let such a thing happen? I don't believe it!'

Rigbi's face was all crinkled up. He was about to burst into laughter, and looking at the bright yellow gravy and the steam rising up off the floor, we were all beginning to feel the same way. Dabo was already spluttering helplessly. Now Omi looked up from the floor and threw up both her hands to her face and started howling with laughter. Rigbi was doubled over, slapping his thighs and laughing and laughing.

'Hah! Ha! Where's the broom? Ah, curse it! Curse you, you rotten fellow. Hah ha ha!'

'Rotten pot!' said Rigbi, keeling over with mirth. His trousers were splattered with meat and his little boy was kneeling close to his feet, blowing hard and scooping up handfuls of the hot gravy into the basin.

'Here, here...Leave it,' his father said, bending down now and throwing some more pieces of meat into the basin. 'Leave the rest, eh? We'll sweep it up.'

The boy stared at him. Rigbi had stopped laughing and for a moment father and son were locked in an intense exchange of shock, disappointment, apology. Then the boy stood up and rushed out with his small face set and inscrutable.

More bottles of wine materialized. I couldn't stop drinking and eating the belladonna berries. It was like a secret addiction. When I finally made my way home, the sky was cold and pale, like a shell. In the west a strange glow seemed to creep in through the gaps in the hills. For no reason I was thinking how wonderful everything was. The golden chance!

Suddenly I remembered the face of the small boy, so sad and set; so attentive, staring at his father, and I thought, Everywhere you go, sons follow in the footsteps of their fathers, whether worthy or not, trying to earn money, find a shelter, make a life.

The golden chance? Who gets it?

Perhaps that is not even the question. It is simply about doing something, and getting the chance to make your own luck.

on stage

▸◂◆▸▸▸

In the village all the youngsters were grouped around the TV. The picture was just clear enough to make out a glittering stage and a group of men and women smiling and singing.

'How lucky they are!' sighed Mimum. 'In another life, perhaps, we will be happy like them!'

'How do you know they are happy?' said Omum.

'Well, just look at them. They are shining and receiving awards.'

Indeed, the singers were bowing left and right and through the static they could hear the sound of cheering and clapping. One of the singers was holding up something and turning and bowing in all directions.

'How clever they are!' sighed Mimum again. 'Really, these ayings have everything. They are too much!'

'In my next life I would like to own a horse and live like a queen!' said Omum.

Mimum burst into laughter. 'Just try it,' she said. 'A fine queen you will make with your short nose and small eyes!'

Omum stared at her, then she said, 'My eyes are my eyes. I may not be a great beauty but at least my eyes are where they should be, and my nose hangs in its rightful place. What more does a human being need?'

Now her eyes were completely shut as her round, childish face puffed out with suppressed laughter.

Suddenly Yayo started intoning, 'What is luck and happiness? Every human being shares the same lot. They may have soft hair and pretty eyes, these plains people, but how happy are they? Who knows, perhaps they are just pretending because they are on TV...'

'How can anyone pretend so much, especially in front of a camera?' said Mimum smartly.

'They can pretend more in front of a camera—why not? Everyone can pretend in front of an audience, everyone knows that,' retorted Yayo. 'That's the whole game. Where you can't pretend is to yourself.'

'Well I don't think so. They *do* look rich! If I had money I would be so happy,' insisted Mimum stubbornly, causing Yayo to snort and say, 'How do you know? You might have all the money in the world but from whom would you buy your happiness, eh? Who has so much happiness that they can afford to sell it to anybody, can you tell me that?'

The TV hissed and spat and the singers started jumping up and down as bands of black and white wavered on the spotty screen.

'Well, there goes,' said Mimum. 'What a place!'

The younger children did not move. Instead they stared harder at the screen as though their concentrated gaze would correct the signals and restore enough power to revive a clear, sharp picture. The dark clouds looming over the hills were of another world. The sound of chickens, dogs, the squealing of the pigs as they trotted around the houses, all these things were far, far away. A large sow came up and stood looking at them, grunting and twitching her tail. Her beady eyes had a hurt and querying look.

'Look at her, shameless!' shouted Omum, and immediately hurled a stone at the heaving side of the pig. She kicked up dust and moved back a few paces, scraping the earth with her trotters.

'Hai! Go away. You've had enough for one day,' shouted Omum again, resolutely turning away. But after a while the silence and bulk of the sow got to her and she rose angrily, 'Come on then, you greedy!'

The pig twitched her snout and grunted good-naturedly to let her pass.

The singers on TV continued their programme, and the group gazed in silence at the distant world of the plains. They stood awed, and faintly envious, on the bamboo floor, by the jackfruit tree, under the rustling thatch, turning their heads only once when the loud singing voices of some boys coming up the hill distracted them.

~

Mona and her film-maker friend came to survey the place, and I travelled around with them, telling them our stories, till I was tired of words and yearned to sit back and only listen. When they left, I was full of energy again and eager to share in the busy rhythm of life in our village.

It was sowing time, and everyone had set to work for the annual fencing of the fields for cultivation. It was a major operation. A vast tract of jungle was cleared and grass and bamboo were set ablaze. The fires burned for many days and nights. Excitement mounted with the leaping flames. The air crackled and the burning debris covered the land with fertile ash. Young men prepared wood and bamboo stakes and fenced the new fields to protect them from grazing cattle and wild animals, making a line of demarcation that could run for miles. It was a great and necessary feat. Everyone looked forward to the end of work and the fairs and festivities that would follow.

Traditionally, the evening after the fence was ready, the party of young men returned home dancing. Dressed in the costumes of warriors they leapt high into the air, slashing and whirling with swords in mock fights. According to the old-timers this tapu dance had originated as a performance to drive away the spirit of fear that sometimes preyed on men. At such times friends and elders gathered and put on their war dress. They fastened tufts of the thorn-wood stem on their shields and spears and made frightening sounds and gestures to scare off the invisible enemy and impart courage to a friend who was wasting away with fear or some sad sickness.

At night the men would dance in the longhouse. If you were absent your friends could steal a cooking vessel or wring the neck of one of your chickens as a fine! The men danced until daybreak and this would be repeated for three nights. On the last night they would dance into all the houses and would be welcomed with food and drink. Everyone agreed that in the old days everything was tastier and the flavour of meat and food more mouthwatering. But it wasn't as if all that fun and flavour was permanently lost. There were still moments of magic and laughter, and every now and then someone would exclaim, 'See, even old woman Neku who never smiles is smiling tonight!'

While the earth slept and nurtured the planted seed, the villages grew animated and sparkled with stories and songs.

This year a crowd was already milling around for the celebrations in Pigo. In the open field near the old market people were talking loudly and settling into the rows of plastic chairs. Some boys were climbing over the new fencing on one side and jumping into the narrow space where their friends were already huddled together, determined to catch the show without tickets. A number of important visitors had arrived, and the stage was being set to showcase traditional culture through the festival that would go on for three days. Yesterday and today would be presented on the same platform; a mingling of old-style presentations and new, modern talent.

Sirsiri, the great singer, was somewhere in-between, I thought. She was neither old nor very young. She had come down from Gurdum, representing Duyang. As usual, she was dressed in a tight, traditional outfit and took great pride in her role as local bride, wife, and mother of sons. Yes, she was intolerable, but the gods had gifted her such a voice that no such celebration would be complete till she had sung her songs. Even her beaten-down husband came back from his wanderings to be with her at such times.

Now we saw her wipe the mildew off her shoes and challenge the bright day as she applied a little powder before stepping out of the Maruti van they had driven down in.

'Is that a new dress?' here husband enquired lazily.

'I bought it two years ago. I just haven't had a chance to wear it yet.'

She meant to taunt him: You don't take me out. You don't entertain. You don't do anything! Other people are doing everything and flying off to the cities and making money and buying cars and gold chains and whatnot!

She stared at their old white van parked in the garden and looked sick with loathing.

'Why can't we have a new dinner set?' she wailed at him suddenly, apropos of nothing, but Pesso was used to this sort of thing.

'Why not? Of course we can! Why don't you get it, but what's wrong with the one we've got, is it broken, eh?'

Sirsiri brushed past him without another word.

She knew it would be different on stage. The crowd awaited her. We saw her step out, swinging her hips and shimmering in the glare of the floodlights. So bold! So confident! She was the one, the woman who knew what she wanted, and how to get it.

This was the thing about Sirsiri. No matter how gossipy and malicious she could be, when she opened her mouth to sing, everything changed. Her brow relaxed. Her beady eyes softened and closed. The abrasive texture of the voice that slandered and whined changed utterly and unexpectedly and became full of whispers, clear and melodious. A note would stretch into a distant wail and tear your heart out as it rose and fell, sometimes a little flawed and faltering but always full of all the pain and longing of the world. At her best she was spellbinding.

How did this strange alchemy take place, I wondered, watching her caught in the pool of light, controlling every trembling strand of music confidently with her thin body swaying slightly, the still hands, the lifted chin, the barely moving lips.

> *Oh, one that I have never seen,*
> *The one that I have never heard,*
> *Who are you?*
> *I send you my name,*
> *In wind-songs I send you my name,*
> *If you do not know it*
> *It is your own fault...*

'More! More!' The crowd shouted.

It was always the same. At this point Sirsiri would gasp and say, 'I can't sing any more. After all, what do you expect? Waah! My children laugh at my voice!'

She had a girl and two boys. The girl was already of marriageable age. 'I had them early, you see. Oh, what a life!'

And she would revert to her mean, scathing self as if there had never been any songs in her life.

When Sirsiri left the stage and the spell she had cast was broken, I noticed there was animated conversation going on in the front rows as the officials in charge nodded and answered the questions of the guests. Then the curtains were drawn back again and the audience saw a woman seated at her loom. She represented the earth. A wide, blue veil was her husband, the sky. Against this backdrop the silhouette of bamboo and giant leaves covering the stage swayed from side to side. Suddenly, there was a sharp crack simulating a shocking thunderclap and a huge, black mithun trotted in.

The angry animal looks around ferociously, his horns catching the sunlight. It is the beginning of the world. He is the firstborn of the earth and sky, and they are still so close to each other that the child of their union is restless, determined to find his own space. While the drums pound and the lights flash on and off across the stage, he tosses the sky away with his horns, high above the earth. The blue cloth is whisked off the stage and all is darkness. Then a pale light grows and spreads and the hushed crowds see the woman standing up now with her hands outstretched to the distant sky. At this point two elaborately costumed figures wearing large discs of the sun and moon appear silently and stand beside her. The earth woman is ashamed and remains standing where she is. A voice, backstage, says: '... and that part of her that was reaching out towards her lord and master, the sky, became fixed forever as the great mountains...'

Everyone in the field clapped and shouted. They knew who was playing the earth woman and the mithun, and they called out the names of the sun and moon and cheered them. It was becoming very lively. After many calls for silence and order the curtain lifted again. It was Menga X, the legendary performer of yesteryear.

The crowd had been waiting. Thousands of people, young and old, were waiting to hear his voice again. He knew this, but his famed lightning energy seemed to be failing him. The stage flooded with light. He looked at the microphone as if it was a strange, alien object that he had not seen before, and when he held it, I could tell that to him it did not feel good to the touch anymore, and he was uncertain if any true emotion could be communicated through the cold metal pitted with holes and fitted to so many cables and wires. 'It is frightening sometimes. Those deep, booming boxes seem to mock me,' he had told me once. 'This is what happens when you let go, when you are out of touch. I must change with the times or shut up and be quiet for ever!'

The crowd screamed. And then he came out of his stupor. He sang at the top of his voice, not meaning to. He tried to caress the microphone and was awkward. His voice echoed back, unfamiliar and unhappy. He closed his eyes.

'But I want the old days back,' he had said to me. 'The days when I was poor and unknown. It was the time my soul sang at its loudest and saddest. It was also the time my soul sang in elation, for the love of a woman... Oh, the days of my youth, the bittersweet kernel of my days! Give me back my gift! Give me back my soul!'

He was crying now, gasping and choking. The crowd saw none of this, and was going wild, a constant wave of noise in which his voice was lost. What was he singing? What did they hear? He spread his legs wide, thinking perhaps that he must posture, use the tricks of stance, gait, a hand across his brow, one foot stamping. Maybe his vision was blurred and he did not actually see the crowd, and only imagined them all sitting there, in the depths of the big field, staring at him, aghast. He had lost it. The gift was gone! Was that what he was feeling again? The crowd was hardly listening, but seemed to be enjoying the experience anyway. I saw Menga X nod softly, taking in his band, the musicians, all of whom were concentrating on their instruments and struggling with the notes. It would never end. They were a team. They had written their names in the wind, and that was it.

The texture and speed of change was visible in strange ways all across the land. A visitor coming to the town for the first time would still see the green hills, the green bamboo and the green river flowing in all directions, but now there were young men on motorcycles roaring across the stones while young picnickers wearing fake fur and woollen caps waved at passers-by. In the run up to the volleyball tourney this year, I heard that the Motum village team had been disqualified because one of their players tried to play holding a bottle of beer in one hand.

While I pondered all this, I noticed there was another stir of excitement in the front rows. Rakut was presenting something to the visiting dignitaries. It looked like a sheaf of papers. He was moving smartly and bowing and smiling. I knew his daughter would be singing next and sure enough the curtain promptly lifted again on four young girls who began singing a sweet, catchy rhyme in chorus.

Rakut passed close by me just then and I asked him quickly what his papers were about.

'Oh, it is a list of all the illustrious sons of this land from British times!'

Rakut had listed the names of his father and his father's father; he had listed Hoxo, his father, and all the other legendary forefathers, and the bloodline of all the men of the Duyang group right down to the present times.

'He believes that if a person forgets, he loses his soul,' Hoxo had said, laughing, when Rakut had performed this recitation for Jules when we were all sitting on the veranda the other day.

'Well, it's a list of names. Maybe it will be interesting, hah, hah!' Rakut said now and moved on.

The girls were still singing in high, clear voices:

Keep the candle burning
Keep one steady light
In the world that's turning
Keep the candle burning...

How strange and moving my corner of the world appeared to me at this moment! There was nothing that I or anyone else could do to keep or change anything. It would all just carry on, for better or worse, and nothing anyone said or wrote would convey that unstoppable process of the mind by which people, simple, old, clever or unknown, will suddenly come up with an expression of their deepest beliefs. And though I was like a stranger to my village, because I didn't live here, I felt certain that no matter what happened to it, if I were granted a visit after an absence of a hundred years, I would recognize it again even if no record of it had survived.

When my phone rang, and I heard my friends from distant cities, their voices sometimes wavered and faded away. At other times the line was so clear, it was as if nothing separated us, and it was easy to believe in the global village. I heard a friend say sternly to her children, or whoever it was that was making so much noise in the background, 'Hey! Keep the volume down! I'm talking to the land of elephants!' and I thought, Yes, this land of elephants, of jungle and river and hard stones. Here the children still stand back and stick their fingers in their mouths. Here Hoxo and Rakut live and remember on a piece of green earth wedged between high mountains and big rivers. Here live people who walk home under the wheeling sky dreaming dreams and waiting to be awakened by the one great passion—nothing else will do...

And in the end what is there, really, to tell? Men and women, the destiny of a race, villages, some symbols, a few people running amuck, a fire, a river, maybe a land of fish and stars...And elsewhere—what is there elsewhere? Men and women, and cities and streets and airports, and a playground for children flanked by high-rises. And perhaps that is all there is, and it is enough.

Everywhere, people like us, we turned with the world. Our lives turned, and in the circle who could tell where was the beginning and where the end? As Rakut often said, 'We are peripheral people. We are not politicians, scientists or builders of empires. Not even the well-known citizen or the outrageous one. Just peripheral people, thinking out our thoughts!'

When I made my way back to Duyang again to hear what the villagers had to say about the festivities, I found it was bustling with people. Smoke floated out of the homes and there was Losi smiling at me and calling me in. Many visitors and relatives had arrived from across the river and it was refreshing to look at their faces and listen to their voices speaking in familiar accents. I pulled up a stool and sat on the veranda.

'Why should we be afraid of change?' Rakut was arguing. 'Change is a wonderful thing! It is a simple matter of rearrangement, a moment of great possibilities! Why should we be so afraid? We all want to be happy, but happiness eludes us as we keep thinking about it all the time. Sleepless nights. Sad, bereft mornings. Then suddenly, for no reason, the blood hums and a feeling of elation carries us through another day! This is how it has always been. We have nothing to fear.'

When Rakut wanted to, he could speak poetry. He was a lover of words, and though he exaggerated wildly sometimes, everyone agreed with him when he said that the divine spirit had given man words to create loveliness. Now he lifted his hands and said, 'Look! Look! The most beautiful thing is that we are all bunched up together on oceans and cities, and deserts and valleys, far apart from each other in so many ways, but we have words, and the right words open our minds and hearts and help us to recognize one another.' Here he clutched his heart and began to mimic again, 'Hello brother! Hello friend! Hello! Hello!'

Everyone laughed merrily and I saw the women of the next house pause in their work to look across at Rakut's performance. They were laying out thread for new cloth and the loom was already stretched out. They were passing the balls of thread back and forth, the blue and the green and the red, back and forth, back and forth.

Hoxo pointed out the green engot plant growing wild near the house from which a green dye could be extracted.

'Everything is available here,' he said.

His little granddaughter peered at us shyly.

'Go and ask grandmother for the big glasses,' he said.

The little girl skipped off and came out almost dragging the big copper-coloured binoculars. I knew Hoxo and his granddaughter often sat together on the veranda and peered through the glasses. 'Guess what I can see,' Hoxo would say, and she would jump up and down and shout, 'What! What!' And he would make up stories and say he could see giraffes and a polar bear, and there, a beautiful snow bird flying over the river towards their house.

Now Hoxo smiled and handed me the glasses.

'Look, isn't it beautiful?' he said, waving his arms across the treetops towards the river.

I held up the old binoculars and peered into the glass. It was a smoky dimness I saw at first. Then I twisted the focus a little and the old lens began to clear and suddenly I saw, yes, a canopy of trees and a river stretching like an ocean with a trembling sliver of light polishing its flat surface. Then, turning the ring a little bit more, I saw, in the distance, narrow apartment blocks, grubby streets, and bamboo scaffolding. I held my breath, mystified, and as I continued to peer intently my sight travelled the horizon and I saw a blue, smoky evening through a window, and through cement walls and through the hills, suddenly, I saw a view of a bright harbour, and sail boats!

acknowledgements

I am indebted, as always, to the encouragement and support of my family and friends, and the goodwill of people I have met everywhere whose generosity made every meeting a happy occasion of discovery. I am also indebted to Ravi Singh, who persuaded me to write this book and who, undeterred by my unruly shorthand, coerced me into greater clarity.